North of Brattleboro

Bruce Hoyt

illustratons

by

Mary Simpson

Railroad Street Press
St. Johnsbury, Vermont

North of Brattleboro

Stories, Poems and Art
With a Vermont point of view.
Bruce Hoyt and Mary Simpson
(Cover: "Lakeland Spring" by Mary Simpson)

Printed in the United States of America

Illustrations by Mary Simpson

LIBRARY OF CONGRESS
CATALOGING-IN-PUBLICATION DATA

Hoyt, Bruce

North of Brattleboro/Bruce Hoyt.

ISBN 9781936711321

Railroad Street Press
394 Railroad St., Ste 2
St. Johnsbury, VT 05819

Table of Contents

Heat Lightning

When the warm night
Had all but folded into darkness
The saw-tooth range of mountains,
New light came.
Thunderheads, too far for hearing,
Arced to violent life
And threw the light
Against a starless sky.
Trees, boulders clouds and man,
Caught in a fraction of their allotted time,
Flashed uncolored in the brief electric flame.
So short its clarity,
And yet so bright,
It showed new destinies
And other paths to try.

The Separation

At dusk , beyond the river, a field on fire
Projected the barren oaks twice into forms forlorn:
Once, as quivering shadows laid out upon the flood.
And once, as death upright
Beseeching still the acrid smoke
Oranged by the fire below.
Among the trees, an awakened house,
With all its windows white with fear,
Stood rooted to the burning field,
Like a wildebeest in the jackal's jaw.
In a town too far away,
A siren wailed an arc of alarm into the night.

The traveler stopping by the roadside to view the scene
Knew that his concern could not bridge the separation
And bring help to the imperiled house.
Shuttering his mind, he slowly drove away,
Following the dark water
Down to other problems in another place.
One cannot always stay to see the outcome of a fire:
To see a house triumphant in the morning light,
Or to see its blackened timbers
Tumbled in upon a smoldering hole.

Starting Over

Into the molding, muddy garden sinks
The last of April's snow. The wintered gardener
Puts away his catalog and thinks
Of flowers and all the bounty he might garner.

Experience tempers optimism, though; crops do fail.
So as he contemplates the stubble and decay
He thinks of drought, coons, cutworms, hail,
Of frost, of gardens lost in weedy disarray.

Yet he recalls the good as well as bad;
Recalls the taste of fresh-picked buttered corn
And firm, red-ripe tomatoes to be had,
And peas. Then eagerly the work is borne.

Getting on with it's the thing
To change the winter into spring.

The Rescue in the Town of Gallant, Vermont

Some time in his later years, my father found a travel magazine of the mid fifties that featured an article about the little town where he once worked as summer farm help. He was convinced that it would be of great interest to folks there and that it ought to reside in the white clapboard library on the edge of the green. He didn't trust the mail to deliver it to anyone who would recognize its importance, so he tried to convince my mother to drive him the 500 miles from our mid-Atlantic city to, as she put it, "some insignificant burg in the New England wilderness." He no longer drove, due to a scary lapse of attention at an intersection. Humbled by this single flaw in his record, he acquiesced to my mother's demands and took the diminished position of passenger. He regained a small portion of his former glory by sliding across the bench seat of our pickup into the driver's seat whenever my mother went into the hair salon or supermarket.

The deterioration that had become evident in his driving failure quickly overtook him and he died not long after. We sang hymns, praised his good life, and heard the assurance of his arrival in heaven. We were politely quiet about the latter assertion but scanned the other possibilities that had been placed in our minds by the diverse cultures of my parents' friends. I pondered the possibility of reincarnation. My mother, who often saw ghosts in the mists of Civil War battlefields, was sure she heard my father's ghost gimping up and down the stairs, looking for his glasses, or rattling bottles in the liquor cabinet, moaning that he no longer had a functioning opposable thumb.

Life quickly went back to a normal routine, but I was left with an extraordinary sadness over my father's undelivered magazine. Consequently, I felt compelled to drive to the "insignificant burg" and deliver it personally. Guided by the calm voice of my GPS I easily found the town in a corner of northeast Vermont, then, could scarcely believe I had found any kind of municipality. You know you are in a small town, when the only store has a porch.

I pulled my beat-up German product in beside a tall pickup, of the same color and make as ours at home, careful not to hinder the exit of the young woman sliding out. Her dress, reluctant to leave the seat before her feet touched the ground, pulled back to her thighs. Agape at this display, I had no time to observe the whole person as she dashed into the store. What I did observe was her dog moving over into the driver's seat and putting his paws up onto the steering wheel. The whole Karma/reincarnation thing came crashing down on me. I understood at once that nagging compulsion to deliver an inconsequential magazine to a far-from-everything town. I got out and went to the truck's open window without any fear that the dog, a golden retriever, would take offense. "Dad," I said, "is that you?" It would be just like him to choose to spend his eternity riding around in pickups with young women. I didn't expect a response nor I did get one beyond the slobbery friendliness that anyone receives from a golden. But I went on with a one-sided conversation, saying, "Dad, I've brought the magazine you wished to have delivered. Hey, and listen, Dad, I've got a great new job waiting for me when I get back. Things are happening for me just like you said they would, Dad."

Things were happening all right. I became aware of a presence behind me that asked. "Are you talking to my dog?" "Are you calling him 'Dad'?" She asked the second question before waiting for the answer to the first.

"No, No," I said, "I called him 'dog' because I don't know his name."

She had to know I was lying but let it go by. "Well, his name is Clyde." She said. "He's been neutered so he'll be confused if you call him Dad." She smiled at her own joke.

Prettiest face I had ever seen. My perspicacity lost its grasp and I muttered "Poor Dad"... dog, dog, poor dog."

She let that go too and stepped up to her truck. Then she stopped. "You've been looking at my ears," she challenged.

I had. Not large, but oddly protruding, and even dangling earrings could not soften the pixie-like appearance that they lent to her appearance. She leaned forward and pulled one of those mysterious wooden pins that women use to sweep up their coiffure. Long, brown hair, with gold highlights cascaded over her ears, around her face, onto her shoulders and down into the scoop-neck bodice of her dress. "So what do you see now?" Actually I saw just a little tip of ear, red with anger, sticking through the hair. But I had seen more than she intended. As she leaned forward, the loose summer dress fell away enough to reveal her considerable contours, accented by a distinct line of demarcation between golden tan and alluring pale breasts.

"Farmer tan," I blurted.

"What?"

"A farmer tan. I drove a pea picker in Wisconsin for a few summers and we were required to wear the company short-sleeve shirt. By fall, I would return to school with a white-as paste body and deeply tanned arms."

"And?"

"And you have one, just not on the arms."

"Thank you for being a jerk," she said as it came to her what I had implied. "Move over Clyde." Then she was gone.

So that's how my first summer after graduate school began. Friendly and impulsive, I let my words slip out unedited and raw, ending a potential romance before it began. I much prefer to write my thoughts, especially in this computer age in which revision can so easily delete an unvarnished thought and replace it with intended meaning.

Ah, well. Nothing to do but to drive into the county seat to find a suitable dinner before returning for the library evening hours.

With the contentment that food and beverage achieves, I felt cheered by the prospect of presenting an important antique magazine to a grateful librarian. All that chilled into uncertainty as I became aware that the only other vehicle in the parking lot was the white truck of the woman who had taken umbrage at my careless words. She was the librarian!

"You've come to laugh at my glasses, the ears weren't enough to amuse you. And that other business about 'the farmer tan'...." I read him out. He deserved it. I'm stepping in to tell this story because if a guy tells it he will make himself right and everybody else will be wrong. If Pirandello can permit six characters to walk in and demand a part in his play, then I certainly can express my opinion. I am Beth and I will tell you about the next encounter.

I don't know whom he was expecting to see, but he acted astonished to find me. He went from glib to tongue-tied and could barely tell me the purpose of his visit. His gift, a very early edition of a travel magazine no longer published, had pictures of our town and its people taken in the late forties. Most of the people pictured have passed on, including my father, who was photographed as teenage helper at town meeting. Nice! We will have the magazine bound and added to our collection. I returned to civility and professionalism. He certainly dressed better than the guys from the nearby state college who room in our village and who come in to study or look for girls. I let up on him and he gradually regained his balance, talking confidently about Vermont authors and poets. Frost, of course, but also Walter Hard and Dorothy Canfield Fisher, indicating to me some connection to our state. He stayed until closing then walked me to my truck, gabbing all the way and, I could tell, choking back some unexpressed audacity. I think I could like him.

I wasn't looking at her glasses. They were demilunes, which I think of as "grannie glasses" but probably right for library work. I was, however, looking at her eyebrows, trying to discern just how their shape made her countenance one of intelligence and yet of caring. Peering over the half glasses in her intention to give me that "what are you up to?" scrutiny, her blue eyes took on a look more sloe and sexy than scathing. She gave me grief for looking at her so intently and again for my happy glimpse earlier in the day. Then she let up and said, "I'm confused. Is the magazine from your dad or my dog?" She smiled a little at her jibe and I melted into a gibbering idiot bereft of any means to make intelligent conversation. I think the meeting went rather badly. I kept thinking of things to say that were too forward for a casual first meeting and that flummoxed the few worthy ideas that might have hinted of an education. That's what comes from being a math major. Still, walking out into the warm summer night with a pretty woman by my side made me feel comfortable about this place. Vermonters, glad to be outdoors without hats and mittens, walked about the square or lounged on the benches by the bandstand.

I am Jay. I forgot to introduce myself back in that first paragraph. Sorry. At birth my name was Jasper. I never liked it and tried being "Jas" for a while. That was mistaken as a nickname for James and I whittled it down to "Jay". My sister's name was Amethyst and she legally changed it to "Amy" when she came of age. Our father was professor of geology at the state university and thought it cute to name his offspring after rocks - excuse me- minerals. Oh, and our last name is "Stone". Thank you, Dad. Anyway, I decided to linger in this village until obligations matured in the fall. I went back to my motel and made plans to stay. Next day I went out looking for a reasonable room to rent.

Now you see there. If they had employed a narrator, these young peoples' attraction for each other would have been explained. I am a narrator. I come from a long line of narrators. Suffice it to say, a competent narrator can tidy up a story and make emotions clear to everyone involved. Here, each actor has an opinion obscura and must wander around in the dark, bumping into misinformation, and postponing the climax to chapter 32. I could have this all done by removing the impediments, getting at least two of the participants into bed by chapter three, and dropping in a hot, sexy scene just before the last chapter. Short book, $19.95 at B&N. A book tour with author in grand mustache and cool threads. Bam! Success! OK, one of my narrator ancestors did stretch a great action story out by inserting a lot of information about melting whale blubber. We have had to adjust to the shorter attention span of modern readers.

I will, however, do my best to build the scenery that sets a mood for this story - for this romance, if I may be so bold.

In the northeastern counties of Vermont, the early days of June stretch the sunlight until after nine o'clock. The sun slides behind the Kittredge Hills, leaving a pale western sky that lingers until a curtain of

deepening blue comes out from behind New
Hampshire's Presidential Range and drapes over the
land. In that bonus hour between sundown and stars,
Vermonters feel excused from serious endeavors and
like to walk around the green looking for the first star
or talking about their gardens. The feeling of well-
being derives from the native ability to forget the bitter
days of January when automobiles groan reluctantly
without starting and roofing nails pop as they contract
in the cold. Jay, having lived his 26 years in the milder
climate of the Mid-Atlantic states had none of that
history, yet everything about the evening made him
want to be in love.

I am Iris. When Jasper… When Jay came looking
for a room I welcomed him as a bit of unexpected
income. The college girls had gone home for the
summer, packing their belongings into one room and
leaving the other unoccupied. I guess I won't have
much to do in the development of Jay's story, but I
have a story I want to tell so I am stepping in.

I am a southern lady and I always will be. I grew
up in Savannah, the most genteel city in America. In
1783, Oglethorpe set up that city in quadrangles of
streets around seventeen garden parks where live oaks
stretch their mossy limbs out over the streets and the
gardens. Stately homes line the outer perimeter, their
floor to ceiling windows, tall gables and double
stairways lending an air of refinement.

I spent seventeen years growing up and learning to
be a refined southern lady- ribbons in the hair, pretty

dresses, perfect manners, all the proper utensils, in sterling, at dinner.

I spent another seventeen years being a wife: Stainless flatware and dinnerware from the catalogs, plus a few pieces of crystal from friends who weren't put off by my marrying before "coming out." My husband was a chemist for a paper company. We had a good life, with money and time enough to enjoy being a young active couple who entertained, traveled, bicycled and even ran the annual race over the Talmedge Bridge. Then my husband, Charlie, got sent to Vermont to run a Georgia owned paper mill. I came too. We bought this old Victorian ark, planning to stay. Then they closed the mill, shipping the major components to Louisiana, and Charlie, too. I stayed here, trying to sell the house and hoping he could find something better. He did. I never saw her, but he was glad enough to leave me that he gave me this house. Divorce is worse than death.

So I spent seventeen years being mad. Not just mad. Vengeful. Every year on the anniversary of the divorce, I go to Burlington to have my picture taken by a professional fashion photographer and have the picture sent to Charlie. I am a good-looking woman, too proud to sink into sullen frumpiness. His floozie, however, is getting fat and bad-tempered. I, on the other hand, can flick a skirt at the guys at the Post Office and they pay attention. I iron my blouses so I look cool and starched while other women are sweating and wallowing in their lack of pride. I wear silky and lacy lingerie that tells me I am still a sexy woman. I get second looks wherever I go downtown, but I don't want the burden of a man. Not Charlie, not Harold at the Gallant Garage, not any of the honest men in this little town who are nice enough to expect commitment in a relationship. If I ever have sex again, it will be casual.

Yikes! That's quite direct. Even as a narrator who likes to get to the action rather quickly, I am inclined to be more subtle. The characters in this story have requested that I limit my duties to setting the scene, so I'll try to do that. Whenever I have had occasion to describe small villages, I have discovered a peculiar insularity in which interest in the affairs of other individuals in the community take priority over the outside world; even more so when a new influence enters the scene . Jasper Stone's arrival in the village, and his subsequent taking up residence in one of the towers of Iris's Victorian mansion aroused the local interest and they watched the light in the new roomer's bedroom as if it were a lighthouse beacon on a craggy coast. Not that they stay up all night. Workers, going down to the "graveyard shift," and those coming back, notice. Those who stop in at The Spile for a nightcap, notice. The driver of the milk truck going up to the farm behind the mountain notices going up and notices coming down. The Free Press comes about 5 am and the driver notices as he tosses out the paper. When lights go off and when lights go on and when lights go off again might be clues to the activity in the house. The basis of this particular avid interest may be found on a shelf behind the second taps at The Spile. On a rather large trophy marking victory in a long forgotten

athletic event, some wag has glued a taxidermy eye
with a prominent blue iris. The "Iris Trophy" will go to
the first man to bed Iris. The trophy is full of money.
Just as there is an annual bet on the exact day and time
that the ice goes out on the local pond, there is an
annual bet on the day and time that Iris will smile upon
someone and take him to her chambers. It hasn't
happened and none of them really thinks it will. But
they like to imagine it. Now, with the new tenant,
twenty-five cent wagers are again filling the trophy.
The money will go to the winning bet and the trophy
will go to the successful suitor.

Mild weather and extended summer evenings
invite the long-wintered Vermonters to come outside
and play. Iris, upon seeing the baseball glove on my
back deck, got out her old glove and invited me to play
a little catch on the street out front. She has a good
throwing arm and put me right to work. *High fly ball.*
"Get under it." *Low and fast.* "Tag the runner coming
to second." *Big throw from right field to home.* "Back
up." Talking continuously and moving constantly, she
showed she could still play the game and trash talk at
the same time. With tight jeans, a Red Sox tee shirt,
and her long black hair in pigtails, she looked like a
schoolgirl. And she played like one too.

"You're a roughneck," I said, "Where did you
learn to play baseball?" Still full of energy from
making me run my ass off, she slipped into another
character and answered, "It was me father taught me,
and he got me a place as the only colleen on the Babe
Ruth team. A longshoreman he was, in the port of

Savannah 'and I'll break their heads if they don't take you on." Me mither was a lidy and didn't approve of my father and me being rowdy and talking like shanty Irish." She rolled her R's like a Boston Southy. She mussed up my hair and we retired to the porch for a Smithwick.

It occurred to me that age is just a number. Sure, it catches up finally but maybe the years between twenty and fifty-something should be considered as a block of healthy living rather than a sequence of decline. Iris is definitely a hot item! Hmm. I turned away from that thought and chided myself for being a bachelor too long.

Escaping from bachelorhood starts with a quest for likely prospects. For a young man, that hunt fires the imagination even before any real quarry is sighted. What might she be like? A thousand poets answer. I once read them all, but when my own words came forth to utter the high romance I felt, they fell to the floor like pizza dough. My evening with that lovely librarian had passed in pleasant chit-chat concealing my desperation to give my very soul to her. I decided to go back.

Restacking books left on the tables by readers and scanners, she seemed taller than in my previous encounters, but it may have been an illusion established by the length of leg she was showing. I did a flashback to the long legs sliding out from her truck on my first day in town. She was wearing a short-hem pastel sun dress of soft fabric that clung to her shape in a most attractive manner. Her brown hair swirled over her bare shoulders in glorious disarray, framing her face like an Alfons Mucha poster. "Good evening Mr. Stone."

"Jay," I corrected.

"Beth," she offered. "Are you looking for something special?"

I was. "Just browsing." I said.

"Let me know if I can help." The professional courtesy left me pondering a dozen opening lines, all of which seemed presupposing or trite. I suddenly realized that I knew nothing about this beautiful woman. In her twenties, she very well could be involved in a relationship already. I explored the little library's inventory then left with a polite "Good night." What a coward!

Other people who were at the library needed my attention so I couldn't open much of an avenue of approach. I had hoped he might offer a meeting after closing. Maybe there will be more comfortable circumstances for him at another time. I will be here serving as librarian until Linda comes back and nobody knows when that will be. She and I graduated in library science at the state university two years ago. She, after several years of piecing together community college and state college, finally took a graduate degree from the university. With my parents help I was able to zoom through in record time. Linda almost ached to get out of town. Who could blame her? Harold's garage doesn't look very prosperous and she hated living in that partially finished apartment above the bays. She received an offer from Boston College and was gone the next week. Harold was devastated.

She bequeathed her job as Gallant Librarian to me. I am quite happy to be here, though I may later try to get in at the state college or at the university. I am living in the summer cottage that my parents stopped visiting years ago. I have a huge garden. Life is good. I just wish the dating prospects could be a little better.

Time to put away the last books. Jay has been busy with the poetry B's. Let's see. Byron. That would be "She walks in beauty like the night of cloudless climes and starry skies…" And Burns. That might be "My love is like a red, red rose…"And here is Gwendolyn Brookes. "When you have forgotten Sundays…" And Elizabeth Browning. "How do I love thee?…" A real romantic. I could like this guy.

I am Harold. I own the Gallant Garage. The sign has been painted over a few times. If you could scrape off the paint layer by layer you could read the history of my business and my hopes. I can tune up any engine or take it down to a complete overhaul, but I can't seem to make much money. Now that Linda has up and left, I don't care much about my finances. I care about my customers and that's about all. I'll drive to all the scrap yards to find parts and take them out myself just to help folks keep their rigs running without breaking the bank. I've put up some plasterboard upstairs and done some painting so the place will be a bit more cheerful for Linda if she ever comes back. I'm pretty low. The only bright spot in my life is Beth and the dogs. When I was damned near to taking the pipe a year ago, she came and said "Harold. You need a dog. A guy came in to the library today and put up an ad for golden retriever puppies. You and I are going to go look." I had kind of tried to put some moves on her a week or two before. I am so ashamed. But she brushed it off as the ravings of a lonely man. Her solution was to buy puppies. She is such a good kid. I could cry for my transgressions. Anyway, brother and sister came home with us. Clyde and Lucy.

I've got to tell you about Gallant. As Narrator I haven't had a chance to say much while these folks are reeling out their own version of events but I would like to tell you why this town evokes so much kindness and forgiveness. It's in the history. At the end of the Civil War, the sons of Vermont had largely disappeared. For the most part, those who were not killed decided against going back to the stony, unyielding uplands and went west to better farmland. One small group straggled back into a wooded section of northeast Vermont not yet given over to sheep. They cut the trees and made a town. At the request of one of the men, an officer, they named the town "Pelham" after his West Point classmate who had left the U.S. Military Academy before graduation and had gone to fight for the South. John Pelham was killed at Kellysville in1863, leading a cavalry charge. This noble gesture of reconciliation was diminished by the somewhat similar spelling of a nearby town called Peacham and the former soldiers took up the gesture again by calling the place "Gallant" in reference to John Pelham's sobriquet "The Gallant Pelham."

Ever since we brought the dogs home Beth and I have met twice a week to let them run. We call it their "play dates." I often take care of both dogs when Beth has something to do and she does the same for me but it's the "play dates" that are important to me. You have no idea how invigorating it is for an older guy like me to be in the presence of a pretty young woman. Forget all the other stuff. Other things were happening that seemed to be omens. This guy came chugging onto the lot with a decrepit Volvo, banging and smoking. He announced himself as "Sutton- no relation to the town of that name."

I am Sutton. First name. Last name. It's what I go by. I got sick of twenty years with a wife who didn't think I ever did anything right. I bought one of the junkers on the dealership back lot and headed out. I had in mind that I might find some rich relative in Sutton, Vermont. I passed through there and kept going. Nobody's rich in Sutton except a few summer people up on the hills with the view. The rest are poor working stiffs like myself. The car was close to death when I came into this burg and found the Gallant Garage. I figured I'd better pull in and not risk this crusher candidate breaking down on the road. Harold, the owner, was kind enough to lend me a repair bay. I can do the work, I just need the parts. Harold is going to let me stay in the old Westphalia out back.

Harold told me I should have chosen a Chevy for coming into the Vermont wilderness. Everybody here has a General Motors "parts car" in the yard or out in the woods, but a Volvo in need is a different matter. People won't let them die, so used parts are scarce.

It may take a few days for parts to arrive. I've had a day or two already with nothing to do but look around. I can't say that I am impressed with Harold's operation. I was repair supervisor at the Volvo dealership in Poughkeepsie and I know a thing or two about customers. You are not going to lure the Audi and BMW drivers into a garage that has a pile of torsion converters in the corner and gobs of used wire harnesses hanging on a post. Driving into this county I saw plenty of pickup trucks and economy GM cars, but I also saw a lot of expensive cars. This is Volvo Valley and Harold is taking up a bay with an old Allis-Chalmers tractor. I'll bet his books show the same business acumen.

A cute young thing just dropped off her pooch with Harold. Too young for him, I think, and definitely too young and pretty for the attention of a grizzled old man like me. Still, there's a bit of a stirring that comes on with the lovely and lithe and it makes me wonder if there is some mature ladies in this town that might give me some of the loving I've been denied for so long.

No time to think about it. I bought paint and rollers. I've started my campaign to transform Gallant Garage. I did a quick clean-up of my crippled Volvo and parked it outside as a decoy. I know all the sources for after-market parts. Customers will be glad to find help without driving to Burlington and paying outrageous dealership rates. I'm excited. Harold is stunned.

I dropped off Clyde with Harold and got a quick introduction to Sutton (first name?/last name?). He looked curious about my relationship with Harold, but it's not something I am going to discuss in two minutes. The less said about Linda's absence, the better, even if it leads to wrong conclusions by town gossips.

Today is farmer's market day at the square. My little garden has produced some peas and some smallish new potatoes, plus a few daffodils. Clyde gets too excited and slobbery with the market crowd so I give him a play date with Lucy and give my attention to my customers. Jay came by, saying that he wanted to buy something to contribute to Iris's table. Seeing me in my bib overalls and my hair up and off my shoulders he said, "So this is how you get your farmer tan." He seemed pleased with this bit of boldness. I feigned a revealing of my tan line. We had a nice little flirt, he bought some daffodils and went off to buy some salad goodies from other vendors. "Where is Clyde?" he asked as he left. "At home with his sister, Harold's dog Lucy." He seemed puzzled by my choosing the words "at home" and I didn't have time to clarify my meaning.

When I saw beautiful Beth in the informal setting of the market, I felt relaxed and bold. She is charming even when selling vegetables. I was entranced by our little tete-a-tete but a bit chilled by the renewal of the feeling that I don't know anything about this lovely person and the other people in her life. That could be a two way street, I suppose. I have been tutoring

Probability and Statistics for two girls at the state college and I haven't been very transparent about that twice-weekly meeting. As very eligible coeds, their presence in my life could be seen as an opening to a relationship. I have kept it quite professional by focusing on the math and trying to fit in the whole course by the end of summer term. A couple of times we have retired to The Spile for a Long Trail or two after our session. It's hard for a young man not to look pleased when escorting a pair of attractive young women into a bar. Those evenings have been very pleasant. Sometimes we sat on the deck out back, watching the Big Bear ramble through the sky above North Mountain. Music and movies and futures and hopes and jokes and laughter passed the evening until the party lights blinked to send us home. Such activities get noticed in Gallant and fixed in minds as romance, though with a good deal of speculation about which girl. In truth, one has a serious boyfriend back home and the other has her eyes on a professor with a Vandyke beard and twenty years of august refinement drawing her youthful ardor.

The inaccessibility of these comely coeds doesn't trouble me. I have had my mind fixed on the librarian with the pixie ears and the winter-be-gone smile. Yet there remains a lot about her that I don't know. I have made sure to visit her booth at the Farmer' Market every week. I went to the library once more to see her and I studied her face in the light of fireworks as the town band played in the gazebo on the Fourth. I saw her one time at The Gallant Garage, bringing Clyde down from Harold's apartment over the bays. I look at her every chance I get and may soon ask her for a date.

Iris was busy tonight with her girls' softball team so I went to quench a thirst and continue my education about this town. Sit at the bar and sooner later one or two talkative people will take adjacent stools. This night only one place was open at the bar: two women on one side and a man on the other side without any apparent business with the couple on his side. I slid in and ordered a Long Trail.

"Al", he said as he extended a gnarled hand to my pencil-pushing, soft-soaped grasp.

"Jay", I returned. "Nice to meet you."

"I am a logger", he said. "Log all winter. Survey woodlots all summer, BS in Forestry, University of Maine."

I told him that I thought I could feel ax, chainsaw and peevee in his grip.

"And chains and harness and fifteen degree cold," said. "I like it. I do selective harvesting and skidding out with a horse. Owners with small woodlots near their homes are willing to pay extra for neat work." He asked what I did for work, so I told him about teaching probability and statistics and showed him a simple distribution that predicts the probability of four boys in a family of four children, or three boys and one girl, or two boys and two girls, etc. Another round and he felt he could ask the question he had on his mind. "Aren't you the guy who has moved in with Iris?"

"I'm the new roomer," I corrected.

"New rumor, that's right. Spelled R-U-M-O-R." He laughed. "You know about the trophy?"

"Yup, and I'm not a contender."

"Well, she is pretty nice. I wouldn't kick her out of bed. We've all been thinking about her ever since she divorced that snot of a husband. She has seethed in anger for a dozen years now. What a waste of a beautiful body. Well, enough of that. Have you seen what that new guy, Sutton something or other is doing over at the Gallant Garage? He goes to Burlington once a week and rents a BMW or Mercedes and parks it outside to make it look like it's there for service. That dumb trick is working and they're pulling in the 45,000-dollar automobiles for 60-dollar oil changes. Harold is fixing up the apartment and hopes to get his wife back."

"I didn't know about that."

"Yup. Harold is married to the librarian, but they haven't lived together for quite a while.

"Harold is what?"

"Married to the librarian and…"

"No! Oh shit! No!"

"What?"

"Never mind. Let me pay the tab. I've got to go."

"Hey, thanks. Nice talking to you."

And that's how the high hopes for my summer ended.

Jay came in late last night. I heard him slam something a couple of times and saw by the lack of light under his door that he had gone to bed without his usual half hour of reading. Next morning, he was furiously pounding in nails on the veranda that

winter's freezes had pulled up. He went from that
noisy activity to hedge trimming and then to edging
and finally, as the sun drew the morning fog and dew
up onto North Mountain, he powered up the mower to
do our lawn, the neighbor's lawn and a strip of the
town green. I enticed him in for coffee and a piece of
pie with a slice of cheddar. "What's with all this flurry
of activity?" I asked. His answer was more of a growl
than spoken words but I was able to interpret it as
"unlucky in love." I dismissed his melodrama, thinking
that, for a handsome young guy like Jay, the loss of
one of those college girls would not be a permanent
injury. More would come in the fall.

He moped around into the mid-afternoon, so I said,
"Let's go for a ride." And added "You're not getting
into my car with all those grass clippings on you. Go
jump in the barrel." A few years ago, I had a cooper in
Jericho make a tub big enough for two people. By
diverting a trickle from the tiny stream nearby, I have a
summer-long "cold tub" for skinny-dipping in the
privacy of my back yard. I couldn't resist the
temptation to take a peek out my kitchen window.
Tight butt. Smooth, athletic body. He won't have any
problem keeping a twenty-something coed interested. I
wish I were a little younger.

By the time I dressed, Iris had uncovered her 1976
Triumph TR6 and folded the ragtop down. We tore off
over to Sutton, then down to South Wheelock, west
over the Stannard Mountain Road to Greensboro Bend,
then down to Hardwick, Calais and finally, to
Montpelier. The TR6 has large wheels so the fenders

come up to the level of the hood, giving it the look of a race car. Iris had given it a racing car workout, bringing us to the capital in time for the last tour of the State House. We had both dressed for the windy ride in sweatshirt and jeans that brought the appearance of our ages closer together. Strolling down State Street, I felt comfortable with Iris. Dinner at the Thrush Tavern, a glass of wine, easy conversation – this had all the ingredients of a romantic evening.

Back on the road again, we crossed over the Winooski River and took the ramp up to I-84. Iris, seeing a long straight stretch of highway, cranked the Triumph up to its magnificent capability and brought us to Waterbury in a flash. Turning north onto Route 100, we eased off and passed through that most scenic corridor, letting the evening shadows of the Green Mountains enfold us. Hyde Park, Eden Mills, Lowell, Westfield, Troy. The windows were dark in all the houses as we left route 100 and turned southward toward Orleans, but the full moon was getting high enough to illuminate barn roofs and white houses. Following our high beams along the eastward road, we pulled into the parking lot for the North Beach at Willoughby Lake just in time to see the full moon peeking into the gap between Mount Pisgah and Mount Hor. Iris had planned this to the exact minute! What a woman!   "Iris,," I said, "I am going to kiss you."

"And I am supposed to do what?" she asked.

"Let me."

"Yes."

His kiss was more than a little thank you for an evening out. There was a passion and hunger that took me by surprise. He held his lips against mine and slid his hand under my sweatshirt, trembling as he touched my bra. Denied for so long, my own awakening was a bit of a surprise to me. Minutes passed in this state, as if something would break if we changed it. At last, he sat back and said, "Iris, I don't know what love is. I courted a woman for four years of college, showering her with gifts and poems but keeping her virginity and mine intact. Then a skuzzy guy with a perpetual three-day growth of beard lured her away. Yesterday, I learned that the person for whom my heart ached was never mine to covet. The trust you give me, the little things you do for me every day and the intimacy that passes so nearby in the kitchen or on the veranda all feel like love to me. I'm tired of being a virgin. Take me home."

That was quite a speech. I started the Triumph and we drove down the lake road under the dark cliffs of Pisgah, the headlights bright on the stands of white birches that line the road. We didn't say anything. Jay helped me put away the car and pull the cover over it. Inside, I said, "Jay, I don't know what there is of me to give, but I will give it to you. Make us a drink. Meet me in the living room wearing your next-to-nothings. I will wear the prettiest lingerie in my drawer. I can't stand ever to be rejected again. It will be all right for you to look upon my body and end this wonderful evening with a kiss goodnight, but if you are pleased with it, you may have it. We'll strip away the packaging and go to bed."

Wow! I've never narrated a story like this. I think my duty here is to set the scene and let the lovers have some privacy. It may be that this little town, nestled, as it is, in the cleavage between matched breasts of rounded mountains, provides a sense of safety and lets its denizens go about the important business of seeing beauty and seeking love. In the pale moonlight coming through the western window, Iris waits recumbent and bare with sheets turned back, her body glowing, and her long, black tresses, coyly laid upon her breasts. Jay knocks lightly and goes in.

I slept like a baby. A couple of times I awoke, but felt so safe and peaceful, that I pulled the covers over my head and resumed the dreams playing through my head. At noon, kitchen noises and the smell of baking bread rose to the room. I slipped on my trousers and made my way downstairs. Iris greeted me by kissing my bare chest over and over, pausing only to say "Thank you, thank you, thank you."

"You've been down here long enough to bake bread?" It was a rhetorical question. The loaves were cooling on the counter.

"Women are different." she said. I've got a dozen years of fire left in my candle and I'm going to burn it like a fire cracker to make up for the years I've lost." I must have looked aghast at this wild woman I had awakened. "Oh, not you. You are excused. It's time for you to go back over to the college and find some young thing you can love for fifty years. It's time for me to find some older guy and love him to death. But I will always, always, always love you, Jay."

So that's the way things stood the rest of the month of July. I continued to tutor the girls and it looked like they were going to pass the course with flying colors. I did take the advice that Iris had given me and sighted a few cherubs that I ought to meet. Still, I thought about beautiful Beth and went each week to the library or the market just to look at her. Wrong, I suppose, to covet Harold's wife but apparently they aren't living together and she's too young for him and, and…and I better go back over to the college and work at something more realistic.

Down at The Spile they had been working all month over the observations about the car and the lights and the brighter countenance Iris was presenting. They expected me to step forward to claim the prize just as any one of them would have done. I just told them that a gentleman never reveals a lady's exploits.

Then, one day, all Hell broke loose. Iris and I were having our second cup of coffee when Sutton arrived with the two slobbery, excited goldens.

"Where is Harold?" we asked. "Doesn't he take care of the dogs on market day?"

"He's locked up the apartment and gone to Newport to the Cathedral. Linda has come home, pregnant. Fell in with some married man. Now she wants to keep the baby…the baby that Harold couldn't father but that Linda desperately wanted. He's gone to pray to St. Joseph about it."

"Where is Linda?"

"Out in my car, crying. "

"Well, bring her in, for God's sake." Beth arrived just as Linda and Sutton came up the walk. The dogs were barking. I was trying to process the information about two wives or two librarians. Iris was trying to explain about the separation. I threw myself at Beth, and cried out "I Love you, Beth! I love you! I love you! Marry me." Linda was sobbing so loudly I could hardly hear Beth's whispered reply "Aren't we supposed to date first?" It was like an Italian opera.

The room hushed when Harold appeared in the doorway.

"Well?" we all said at once.

"Joseph said that I will get use to it."

And I did get used to it. I grumbled a bit and then got interested in what was going on inside Linda's big belly. When the little boy arrived, it was *my* little boy. As soon as little Hal could grasp a finger, his proud Daddy presented him with a small, silver-plated crescent wrench.

Beth and I did date, spending every minute we could, together. One August day we hiked up to the top of North Mountain so Beth could show me, that from the summit, one can see all the way to Egypt. I had forgotten that the one village with a name other than something-or-other Mill had the exotic name of the land of the pharaohs. I wrestled her down for her bad joke, then stuffed wildflowers down her bra. We might have made more of that, but it began to rain. The rain turned into a downpour and we slipped and stumbled down the muddy trail, arriving at her house looking like a pair of last-place cross-country runners. "You take the upstairs shower. I'll take the downstairs. Just leave your clothes on the floor and we'll throw them in the washer a bit later. My father's old robe is in the closet. You can wear that."

When I came down, she was lying naked on the broad cushioned window seat. There was a smile that showed her delight at putting me off balance, and then there was a smile that was an invitation to intimacy. I shed my robe and went to her. Our caresses fell into the rhythm of the rain on the metal roof and we floated through an unhurried dream until the rain stopped and the sun came out. The peculiar light wove gold threads through her hair.

"It's a rainbow," she whispered. "There will be a rainbow on the other side of the house. Stay here, though. There will be other rainbows to admire."

"But only one treasure," I said.

I will write the last chapter of this story, because it ends, as it began, with some of Jay's crazy perceptions. A package came today and I opened it. Understanding its significance, I took out the object and set it on its box in the hall. I heard him come in.

"Oh, shit!" he declared.

"Little ears, little ears," I warned. Actually, our Amy has prominent ears like mine. Jay wouldn't hear of surgical correction. "She's beautiful," he had proclaimed, and that was that. "The package is from Ira and Iris, Mr. and Mrs. Ira Sutton," I shouted. "The patrons of The Spile awarded the "Iris" prize to Sutton and then gave him all the quarters as a wedding present. Iris made Sutton send the prize to you."

"But…" Jay stammered.

"But, now you think I know something I didn't know before? Iris told me that summer. She told me you were a great lover and that I had better rescue you before you got lost. Besides, the score is Iris, 1: Beth, about 216. Make that about 217 after Amy goes to bed."

Jay sighed. "Glad to help." Then, to Clyde, he said, "What do you think of that, Dad?"

Round-up in the Supermarket Parking Lot
(An Urban Cowgirl's Lament)

A dozen times today I've rounded up these wandering carts
And saved them from destruction, theft and weather.
Though herdsman I may seem,
I speak no pretty metaphor of husbandry;
If more than steel and plastic these may be,
Then they are just the witless analogs
Of my life's perennial chaos.
Here on this cold and snowy macadam plain
I've struggled every day to make reason answer entropy.
I've soaked my shoes and mashed my fingers.
And I've battered every corner of my soul
Trying to hold back the galloping fragments of disorder.
So once again in gaudy orange costume
I go forth to conquer,
While, safe behind the glass,
God and the manager look mildly on.
You there! Impatience,
Rattling empty down the cobbled mall,
You'll be the first inside.
I'll nest and chain you in Frustration, where you'll stay.
And Error, too,
I'll try once more by strength and will
To dominate your skewed-wheel deviations,

Great and small.
And, oh again, Loneliness:
Will you always be abandoned in the road?
Hurt, Anger, Fatigue, and Doubt,
I'll gather you up and hide you all inside.
Now all together,
Clustered,
Rolling,
Clattering,
Charging toward the door.
I will not hear your whining protests.
In you go!

Rap Song for a Vintage Volkswagen

The quarter panel's rusted
And the headlight cowling's busted
And the floor pan's almost dragging in the street.
The muffler sounds like thunder
And the bumper's folded under
And the heater's blowing cold air on my feet.
I think the time has come
To junk it out.

The upholstery is tattered
And my girlfriend isn't flattered
When I call to take her for a ride.
The gas gauge works just partway
So she 's pushed a league of parkway
And she's wondering when I'll get some pride
And junk it out.

The accelerator's sticking
And the second gear is kicking.
The back seat's full of junk that should be tossed.
I've got a chainsaw, ax and spare tire,
But the trunk's tied down with haywire
So my chance of getting at 'em 's all but lost.
You can understand why I might want to
Junk it out.

Where there's paint it's blue and hazy.
Where there ain't it's rusted lacy
And one fender's flapping in mid air.
Every side has had its mishaps.
There's no tread upon the recaps.
And the engine... well the engine, let's be fair:

Starts at thirty-eight below.
Reg'lar gas will make it go.
Just a bulldog in the snow.
I don't know...
Maybe Bondo^{tm}.
I think I should consider
If a little work will rid her
Of a blemish or an irritating trait.
It's getting cold for biking
And I'm not fit for hiking
And I'll save a lot of money if I wait
Before I junk it out.

Junk it out?
Junk it out?
I might not be in style

But I'll go another mile
Before I get around
To junk it out.

di Suvero

On misty days
Marc di Suvero's iron tribute to his father
Stands strong against the outline of Storm King
Mountain,
Its dark "I" beams recalling Franz Kline's black
diagonals
On stark-white canvas.
Solid as the mountain,
The sculpture carries a cable-hung wing of steel
Appearing weightless enough to fly off over the
landscape
To the Hudson River.

Our own di Suvero took a corner of the campus
Dominated by the Baker Library,
Its iron bones supporting a chain-slung palette;
A whimsical swing
Befitting the college scene.

One late night as we came from the Union,
A heavy fog rolled up from the river
And blurred the library's window-light to a diffuse
glow.
Against this backdrop, the massive iron thing
Revealed the true intentions of the artist,
Showing strong black diagonals against the whiteness
Of backlit fog.
We climbed aboard
And swung the groaning planks to action.
Amazingly,

The iron beams loosed from their concrete footings
And lifted us over the increasing fog
Carrying us over the globes of light around the green,
Over New Hampshire's mountains,
Over the ocean
And across the continents
To an ancient land
Where we were clothed in silks and wisdom.
Venus was in the morning sky when we returned.
We took off our shoes and climbed down
To walk barefoot home across the dew-glistened green.

Sunfish

Upon the waters once, before I met you,
I sailed those foggy banks beyond the Flemish Cap.
There, the cold currents sweep the great ice from the
Davis Strait
And sink beneath the warm Gulf Stream
To stir that northern sea to green life;
A pasture for whales.
Half a day's steaming, though,
Will take a ship to where the hypnotic clarity
Opens the depths to all who peer into it.
A decade later on an inland lake,
We danced our little boat upon its beam-ends
And felt the wind caress our backs.
A lively northern breeze wedged up a bank of
thunderheads,
Bright in the early day,
But later pink and glowering against our progress up
the lake.
I watched your eyes, blue-green like those northern
seas,
Searching the wind and weather.
With rapture like the divers trap, I sank into their
depths
Until a flash of wave-mirrored sunlight broke the
trance.
I let fly the sheet and held you for a little while,
Rocking,
Drifting,
On a summer lake.

Rowing

Magdalena, gorgeous girl, you taught me how to row.
"Just watch my back," you said. I did, and that is how I
know
Your form is like a statue, but supple, soft and tan;
A hundred times I flexed toward you each kilometer
span.
The legs pull up and push away, and the back bends to
the oar.
We thought that we were Vikings heading for the
Greenland shore.
But rowing's mostly rhythm; the coxswain told us
what to do.
On those stretches up the river, I was free to look at
you.
You wore your hair swept up; brunette, like swan's
down at the nape.
And on your neck, a golden chain adorned its classic
shape.
Our coed "eight" went out each day in foul or sunny
weather.
Quite soon I learned to drop my wrists to bring my
sweep to feather.
We rowed through scenery idyllic
Listening to the coxswain's chant dactylic;
"Pull... two, three, pull... two, three, pull... two,
three."
It was waltz time on the water: My heart danced when
you smiled at me.
 Etes vous prete? We thought we were. Seven miles
we'd rowed each day.

But a race calls up all that you can give before you put
the boat away.

So when we left the boathouse, we flopped down upon
the shore.

And sad, I knew, at summer's end, I would not see you
evermore.

The Parkway

Down to the city
Early in the year
And early in the morning
The trees along the parkway
Stand black against the white dawn sky,
Stand black against the silver river
Reflecting the white dawn sky,
Their silhouettes establishing identity
That will be lost in summer green.
Here, a maple with its opposite branching,
There, an oak with its sturdy alternate stems,
Over there, a beech with twisting limbs,
Each appear as if alone in dendritic distinction.
Opposite gives rise to opposite,
Alternate to alternate,
Twisting to twisting,
Each junction giving rise to multiple junctions
Further from the trunk,
So that the shape is softened by the finer twigs
Which know how to end
Within the predestined shape
Of oak or maple or beech.
Fractals, one might say.
Not so neon bright,
But still akin to those self-similarity patterns
On the Mandelbrot posters and tee shirts of the
nineties,
Where each figure was edged with multiple repetitions
Of the original
And those were likewise edged,

And so on,
Melding the parts into something new.
The branching becomes the tree.

Here now in sight
Is the obelisk,
Here are the towers, columns, arches and domes
Here is the engineered geometry of the man-made
world,
Bright in the morning sun.

Upper Valley Airport

The summer when we tried to fly
Our farmer pilot led us to an outer shed
Where an ancient high-wing Cessna
Stood humbly on its triangle landing gear
Inside walls with posters of Citabrias.
Wheeled into the sunlight,
The aluminum airframe seemed eager
And bright
And aerobatic enough
For us fledgling flyers.
With little spare cash in those days
We did rock, paper, scissors
And you were the one to fly.
You climbed aboard,
And took your place beside the farmer/pilot.
The engine came to life,
Roaring at first,
Breaking the grip of friction and inertia,
Then, whispering competently,
For the plane to taxi down the lawn-smooth
Grassy runway
And turn into position.
The engine roared a protest
Against the momentary hold of brakes.
Released, the little plane gathered speed
Down the narrow strip
Between the fields of quivering corn.
You smiled at me through the noise
As the plane lifted gently into the air.
I wished you well

Out over the meadow and the power lines,
Out over the river,
Out over New Hampshire's mountains.
And I wished you in the tiny speck
Reappearing under the clouds,
Flying back to me.

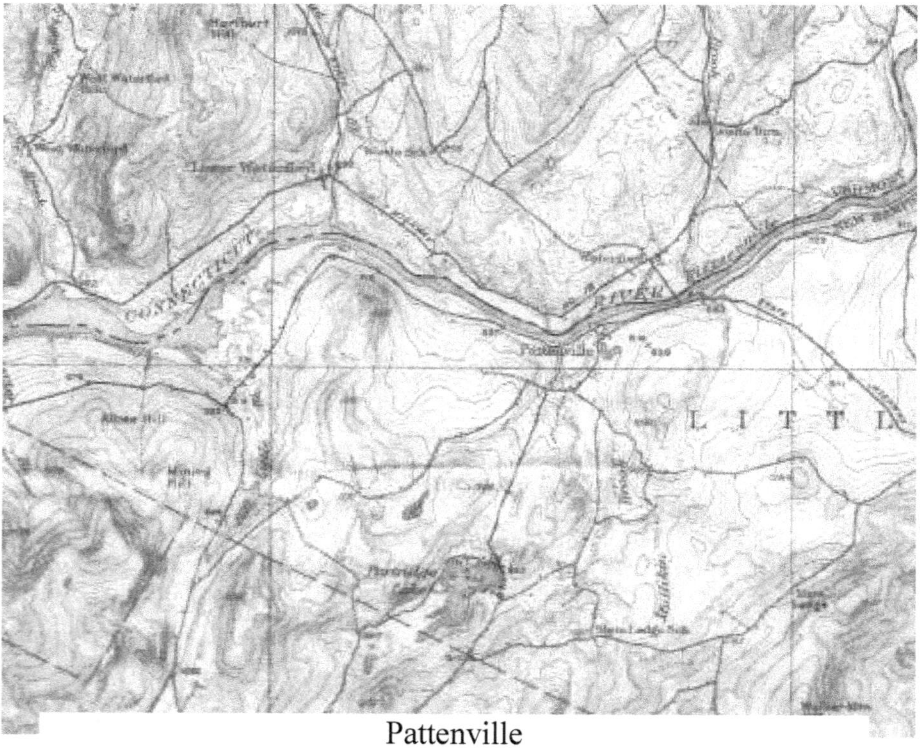

Pattenville

Remembering Pattenville by the Connecticut

Some time ago I received a letter from a longtime friend explaining his sudden departure from the St. J. area. I will relate his frightening story but will limit the details to protect his privacy.

When the Moore Hydroelectric Station was under construction in the mid fifties, many of my contemporaries took jobs vibrating the tons of concrete in the continuous pour. The letter writer, however, hired on with a crew moving remains from the old Pattenville cemetery up to higher ground. The village, if it could be called that, consisted of half a dozen houses where route 18 swooped down through a valley. It would eventually lie beneath 170 feet of water, necessitating the removal of its buildings and the bodies resting in its graveyard.

College age students, supervised by a funeral director, used hand tools to disinter the deceased and carefully placed the remains in individual, labeled boxes for transfer to a new resting place.

The temptation to take shortcuts comes to us all at one time or another and for my friend it came late on a Friday afternoon when he was tired and more than ready to finish up and get back to the temporary dormitory that housed the young workers. A body in particularly advanced decomposition was going to require a lot of sifting and picking. He had heard that moving a difficult grave could be accomplished merely by moving the soil reddened by the iron-rich, decomposed liver of the deceased. So that's what he did.

My own compliance to the easy way came that summer when I painted the Portland Street Overpass with a steeplejack crew. The boss said the "pigeon poop primer" would be adequate in the hard to reach (and hard to inspect) places. Good enough for me!

My friend, however, soon saw his shortcut as a desecration and a sin. We'd talk about it over a brew from time to time, and the pain in his conscience gradually subsided. It reemerged sharply a couple of years ago when he took a job in Littleton. Every workday he had to drive by the sunken foundations and vacant graves far below the reservoir surface. He knew what was out there.

No backyard tree or TV antenna pokes the surface to mark the place, but Pattenville lies beneath the south tending cove of the lake that comes near the arcing I-93 highway, just beyond Moore Station. On late summer nights, the warm water and the cool air above it tends to generate fog. For him, the fog generated unexplainable forms which gave him such anxiety that he often stopped for a drink before heading home. The forms became a bearded man with soggy clothes and straggling waterweeds. The drinks became harder. Once, as he drove by, the apparition shouted "I want my…"

My friend gunned his Dodge up to red line and never heard the rest. Thereafter he always drove with the windows up. He didn't have to hear it, but still he saw the vision more and more through October. It gave him a burning sensation at the bottom of his rib cage. Finally, he wrote in his letter that he had to move away to another state to find a new job and avoid this torment. A month later he was dead.

We all had our suspicions, so a nurse in our group made a few phone calls and reported back: "Yes, cirrhosis." Then added "not the usual spongy form of liver deterioration, but more like burned, cooked".

A couple of the guys said, "Yup, drank too much." One offered, "Microwaves. He worked on microwave towers." Another remembered taking his girlfriend out to see the new hydro station, and seeing an old man trudging along the bank, as if looking for something. " I felt a pain in my gut and a chill at the same time", he said. "Creepy! I never went back".

We talked some more about these strange phenomena. There was even a proposal to go see for ourselves but we decided that we would look ridiculous. We're all too old to go "sparking" in the moonlight, so we ordered another round and left the matter to be explored by younger guys and their girlfriends. If they dare.

Bede's Sparrow

Out on the road
A hiker,
With cardboard destination-sign half held in shivering
hand
Like a dubious talisman before the scathing headlight
glare,
Pauses,
Regrets once more his ill decision to cut across the Y
A few miles from the junction of the turnpikes
And trudges on.
But in the vanishing-point
Toward which the shrinking tail-lights hasten
He visualizes, more than sees,
A diffuse, not-quite glow,
Which his hope and quickened pace
In time unfolds from the curving road
As light,
As extravagant radiance laid like a carpet
Over the snowy road.
There,
Under blue stars wincing at the unrelenting cold,
A tiny all-night diner gleams a promise
Through a line of frosted windows.
A warm place at the counter.
Coffee.
Dishes clattering in the sink.
The smell of tomorrow's pastries, baking.
Talk of the record cold,
Of the high cost of fuel,
Of the friend dying, probably by March,

Without seeing apple blossoms on the trees he planted
For a child whose name is lost in kitchen sounds.
A last bite savored,
A smile,
And with the counting out of change, a wish bestowed.
He sees, upright, the hands upon the clock.
Through the long window in the door
He sees Orion, upright, crossing the meridian.
He hesitates in the burst of cold air
And vanishes into the dark winter from which he had
emerged.

*The present life of man, oh King, seems to me in
comparison to that
which is unknown to us, like the swift flight of a
sparrow through the
 room where-in you sit at supper in winter with a good
fire in the midst
whilst the storm of rain and snow prevail abroad; The
sparrow flying in
 at one door and immediately out the other,
 whilst he is within is safe from wintry storm but after a
short space
of fair weather immediately vanishes out of your sight
into the dark winter from which he had emerged.*

from Bede's Ecclesiastical History, 731 a.d.

Remembering Route Three

He would not die.
Even in the Boston hospital when he looked up,
Frightened, questioning,
From a bed saturated with his own vomited blood,
He would not die.
The family huddled in the shadows of the room
While white uniforms moved about under the harsh
light
Something undefined, uncontrolled,,
Burned inside his sunken body
And had surely finished him at last.
But he would not give in to it.
He would not die.
Then, at his request,
He moved toward home through a black night
Splashed with a monotonous repetition of red
Pressing numbly against the ambulance window,
And sliding back into the miles behind.
No siren disturbed the midnight road,
But the dim sterility inside was pierced with his agony,
As each bump and turn goaded his body.
Like unimportant stars spaced by lightless ether,
Chelmsford passed, and Tyngsboro and Nashua
He coughed a crying, tortured cough,
And tried to talk.
He grasped the rails of the litter
And drowning, delirious, clung to life.
Construction on the road from Manchester to Concord
Evoked his weakened cries,
But could not kill the body which the Depression

Had transformed from slender clerk
To barrel-chested, muscular grain carrier.
In the winding road to Plymouth
He lurched back three decades and howled again
His frustration against a spring flood
And a bridgeless chasm in the road.
The road of horrified flight away from a blundering
doctor,

He could not earn.
He could not control.
He could not die.
Nor could he die that morning, years before,
When he found his father with chest blown open
Slumped over his shotgun in the woodshed.
Lincoln, then the dark mountains of Franconia Notch
Drifted back through the night.
The pain would not let him stay with the present and
reality.
Pushed back to other anguish,
He argued again and again with his mother,
Trying to save something of his own worth.
He would have died then,
But could not.
The ambulance bore on,
Unremarked by the stone profile in the ledge.
The driver cheated curves and tried to make the ride
easier
Down through Mittersill to Franconia and Littleton.
But the old road was abandoned to hope of Interstate
And riddled with potholes of neglect.

It yanked, twisted and rolled
The suffering body until it came apart from his tortured
mind.
He became strangely lucid as the vehicle raced through
Waterford
Lights in the barns marked the hour.
He tried to see the new day and rose slightly.
He began to remember out-loud a morning in Maine
When fishing with his son, they came upon an old
burn,
Grown to a lush garden of blueberries.
Like greedy, frenzied bears just out of hibernation,
they picked and ate.
Then, giddy in the extravagance, made containers of
their shirts
And filled them with berries, leaves and twigs, all
hastily gathered.
They ran half crazed but triumphant
Before a cloud of no-see-ums that chased them all the
way back to Rangely.
He laughed and gave up consciousness.
The ambulance wailed its way through St. Johnsbury's
intersections
And turned toward the hospital.
He would not die for three more days.

Bicycle

My freedom's sleeping in an outer shed,
Held high above the floor
As gently as a dancer in a dream of prolonged flight.
Her delicate frame waits patiently for me
To awaken her and let her down.
When her firm, thin tires touch the ground,
Bearings, ratchets, gears all quicken,
And she sings a soft metallic song
As she remembers the fire, sand, mill and lathe
Of her exquisite birth
And as she anticipates the black macadam ribbon
Of her joyous life.
Wheeling into the morning light, she brightens.
And the gray, metallic luster of her slender body
Beams a promise of adventure and delight.
Her chromed arms sweep forward,
Articulate in fingers of control,
And turn back again to give a taped grip,
Warm and unreserved
Into my hands.
Leaning together a moment, we two become a rolling
one
Consummate in our motion.
Now climbing in low range up the first section
Steep and long and slow, with labor,
Then cresting, shifting, gaining, free,
        Take me away from cares and clamor.
        Take me to a life I see.
        Clicking the gears up faster and faster

Our sleekness slices the wind
A blur of spokes flashing at heaven
Daring dull gods this swift love to rescind.
Motobecane,
I know you can
A vision pursue,
Take me with you.
Take me away.
Take me far away.

Herding Sanderlings

Through the dunes and down to the beach
As the morning sun shines green through the breaking
waves,
I come to the spilled foam where little birds
Pursue the ebb and flow of ocean water on the sand.

On the beach,
The workday thoughts give way to lighter musings
And I consider the possibility that on the Fifth Day,
Around three o'clock in the afternoon,
God said to his angels
"I'm tired of working on this 'Man' thing.
Trying to make him in our image seems perilous.
To infuse a creature with freewill like ours
May lead to purposes that are not in our intention.
Let's give it a rest and start again tomorrow."

Not content to rest,
The angels brought forth a design for a silly little bird
That runs on swift black legs,
Bobbing
And poking the shallow water with its long beak.
God laughed and said, "Let it be so".

And there they are, in two's and three's
All up and down the strand.
But as I walk along,
Barefoot in the shallow water,
The two's and three's become four's and sixes
And without so much as a "whoopee-ty-iyo"

I become herdsman to two-dozen sanderlings
Pushing on ahead, with none behind me.
The density of this grazing herd increases until,
All together,
They assert their will
And take to the sky in a gray flutter
And wheel in the air to show white underbellies
Like a cluster of blown papers,
Scattering to land up the beach behind me.

High Wire

Come walk the wire with me
Above the numbed gray faces and their trodden earth.
Alone and free,
In golden light,
We'll dance away dull reason's dreamless gravity
And fill our lives with stars.
Audacious dancer, leap with me
And laugh at those who hope we'll fall.
Dance, leap, love and laugh with me
In the magnesium fireworks of this moment
Far above Earth's sweating hold.
We live in air presuming upon a floor of light
And yet,
I cannot stay.
I cannot claim this piece of sky
And hold this radiance within.
But when I must go down
Into the stifling shadows where the rasping voices are
Ill tell them what we dared:
I'll say that on a cosmic thread
Too high for any tent to hold
We sang our hearts and danced our dream
And in the summer night, heard Orpheus' golden lyre.

Magic Chair

With button eyes watchful and fuzzy ears alert,
And ready for the journeys they might take
A bear in a hat and a borrowed green tee shirt,
Waits in a chair for the dreamer 'til she rises.
An indefatigable, fiber-filled bear,
Sits in the roll-about second-hand office chair
With built-in fantasy and wonderful surprises.

With her magic chair
And her loyal bear
The dreamer can go anywhere,

As punakawalla bear to a raja in the Pradesh
When the chair was in the Delhi Embassy,
He told the dreamer that his master liked horseradish
Which she served on soybean wieners with supreme
diplomacy.
(To the handsome prince
Whom she writes to since,
Though their friendship still is veiled in secrecy.)

With her magic chair
And her loyal bear
The dreamer can go anywhere.

When her bear was a boatswain on an old Liberian
freighter
And its rusting hull split open in a gale,
She radioed position as they all slipped underwater.
And her strength was just about to fail

But still she rescued Bear
Then up popped the chair
And she pulled them all on board a passing whale.

With her magic chair
And her loyal bear
The dreamer can go anywhere.

On the treacherous Khombu Icefall with her sturdy
Sherpa bear
And Lhotse towering over and Everest up ahead,
The climber slipped, the bear belayed and snubbed her
in mid air.
With ice chunks falling 'round them they looked down
with shiv'ring dread
And though they lost their back packs
Bear still could use his ice ax
And he carried her to Thyngbok to recover in her chair.

With her magic chair
And her loyal bear
The dreamer can go anywhere.

Now the girl is older: Should her fantasizing end?
The bear doesn't think so and stands ready for a flight.
He guards the magic chair for his dreamy, lovely
friend
And he keeps away "impossibles" that hover in the
night.
Why should she to reality be bound

When much adventure can be found
By lying on a fluffed-up pillow and turning out the
light?

With her magic chair
And her loyal bear
The dreamer can go anywhere.

Someday soon she'll go to college
With Emeritus Professor Bear.
They'll roll up to the doors of knowledge
To Einstein, Euler and Voltaire,
To ancient times or ocean depths or even outer space
She knows that she can go 'most anyplace
In her marvelous magic chair.

A dreamer can go anywhere
With a loyal bear
And a magic chair;
A roll-about, tilt back, whirl around, marvelous magic
chair.

Flower-Power Face-off
(Remembering Vera Whitney)

One day a museum visitor showed up
With plant in newspaper rolled up.
With sockless shoes and uncertain beard
He said, "This plant is something weird."
Hoping to embarrass someone over thirty-five,
He showed the saw-tooth leaves, exactly five.
"You wouldn't know what this is, would you?"
The herbarium folder was in her hands before he could
count to two.
'T would be unknown before his generation he was
sure.
The folder opened; "Marijuana, Waterford, nineteen
hundred four."

Dear Brother, Dear Sister

****

October 2005
   Dear Robert,

   Belated thanks for all the letters you wrote to share
your family with me during my enlistment. I didn't
write much because there is only so much you can say
about repairing C17's. Now I seem to be having a life.
I have a nice apartment up over the equipment shed at
the mountain. I get free skiing just for keeping an eye
on things during the night and during the off-season.
My big window looks north toward Willoughby.
Fishing and canoeing are available nearby on the East
branch of the Passumpsic.
   Also, I am hockey coach for a team of beginner
boys (5 to 7 years old). We skate at the new rink
downtown, but I also have a piece of flat ground out by
the willows and I think I will flood it some cold night
and build my own practice area. Maybe get a net.
Come see me. We'll tip up some brews down at The
Outback.
   Brian

   Hello to that cute wife of yours.

****

Thursday, October 6, 2005
Dear Brian,

If I come to see you, it will be only after I send Ginger safely to Alaska, because you probably would jump in your car and try to resume the courting you interrupted when you went off to the USAF. Mine!

Robert
Ginger says "Hi"

****

16 October 2005
Dear Robert,

Not to worry for a while. I am courting a pretty thirty-something, the single mom of one of my players. She goes to bed quite easily. She's lonely. Neither of us has really explored the other as person, but this is uncomplicated pleasure, unlike the Air Force where the interesting women were either married or a couple of ranks below where I could decently pursue them.

One small negative in this present relationship: The son heard us discussing whether or not the mom could be considered a "cougar." The son heard us out of context, thought it a great name for our team and convinced the others. We couldn't talk them out of it without explaining the implications. We are the "Cougars." Son and mom are leaving soon for the mom's new job in DC. I will keep in touch, but nothing much is going to come of it.

Brian

****

Tuesday, November 1st
Dear Sister April,

No job here yet. I hope to get by with an adjunct
position in the math department at the state college for
next term. No social life either. Maybe I should have
stayed home to sink into boredom with husband Jon.
We never did anything there either. Might as well stay
here and do nothing. Sorry to sound so sour.

I kind of live an ersatz romance life by picking up
books at the library and reading them up in the
bleachers at the hockey rink while a beginner team
practices. Ice reminds me of those hard but satisfying
figure-skating practices, back in the day. The coach
has a nice build and cuts smooth turns on the ice. He
skates by me but hasn't really noticed me.

Love, June

****

1

November 2005
Dear brother Robert,

My cougar sweetie has gone, so it's back to a
monk's life for me. There's a good end-of-the-day
crowd at the upper lodge, but the bar closes early and
everybody goes home. There is a young woman who
comes to the rink each practice day, and I can't place
her as a parent, though she leaves when the kids leave.
Kind of pretty, but she keeps her face buried in a book
so I haven't had a good look.

Hoping for an opportunity.

Brian

****

Thursday, November 3rd
Dear sister,

I met the coach face to face tonight. I was
immersed in my book and didn't notice that the kids
were gone and the Zamboni was already parked. He
came over and said, "Excuse me ma'am." He sounded
like he had stepped out of a western movie. "The kids
are all gone and I've got to shut off the lights and lock
up. No more teams tonight." He walked out with me
and seemed to want to talk. I walked slowly to let a
conversation flow. "So what are you reading that takes
you so far away from the real world? " "It's a romance
novel." "I never read one. What 's the premise of this
story?" "Young, exotic dancer wins a fashion
makeover and decides to take her life to a higher plane

by going to college. She is hoping to pass calculus by getting the professor into bed." "At 120 credits to graduate, that's a lot of bed time." "No, no, someone will come along who is more interested in her virtue than her body." He held the door for me and said, "Good night. Come again." I will. I definitely will.

Love, June

****

Thursday, November 10
Dear April,

The little hockey players had a scrimmage tonight. I stayed and helped the coach pick up the wrappers, cups and popcorn bags. We introduced ourselves – he is Brian, recently back into the civilian world from the Air Force. He invited me for a beer and late snack at The Outback. I tried to find out if there are other women in his life and asked about the team name. "Aren't cougars more of an Everglades creature, and not associated with winter sports?" "Oh no. These are snow cougars, pure white and only a little bigger than a cat. There are only a few left in the country and most of them are here, concentrated up near the black diamond ski trails. They really are a lot of trouble, leaping out of the woods to attempt to scare skiers out of their domain. We don't say much about it in the village. The EPA would come in here to protect the 'endangered species' and make…" I interrupted him and said, "There's an older woman in all this hokum, isn't there?" He's such a bad liar. "Well, that too," he said. I smiled at his outrageous story and then we had an honest conversation about each other's lives. I like him.

Love,

June

****

10 November 2005
Dear Robert,

Tonight after our scrimmage, the woman who has been using the bleachers as a reading room stayed to help me clean up when everyone else had gone home. I invited her out for a snack and brew at The Outback. We took a table, which, like the others, augmented the subdued light with a candle stuck in a Jim Beam bottle. The warm light let me really see her for the first time. A blonde sweep of hair across her forehead, around her ears and down to her shoulders, framed a beautiful face. No Modigliani with skinny face and small mouth, this girl has a broad smile that rounds her cheeks and pushes them up to make her eyes seem to laugh. Her generous brows and long lashes enhance her blue eyes. I couldn't stop looking at her. We had a good talk. She apparently is a figure skater of some note, skating as a single and with a male partner to win a few contests over in New York. That may explain her attraction to my ice at the arena. She calls herself a 'liberated female", running away from a dull, overweight husband. I'm giving that a bit of space, but she is incredibly attractive.

Brian

Friday, December 2nd
Dear April,

Brian and I have been seeing each other quite often. He bought me pair of short skis and has been helping me navigate the bunny slope. We visit the nightspots in the two little towns. He has taken me to Burlington on days he works at the airport and, can you believe it, put me up in my own room at a hotel after our evening out. We have a lot of fun but he seems to be holding me at arm's length, very respectful of me, as if I might run if he put some moves on me. I'm not a schoolgirl, for cryin' out loud! One night at The Outback, I pressed him on this. The conversation went something like this:

Me: "According to your theory of love, if a girl –a woman - desired a hug, you would give her one?"

Brian: "Remember that I said if she has an attractive face, one that shows warmth, intelligence, mystery, an inner self to be explored. Then, yes."

Me: "And if she wanted a kiss, would you give her one?"

Brian: "Same answer, more or less, but she would have to signal that desire."

We've already been that far. His affection is sincere and I can tell that he is hungry but reluctant to warm things up, unsure if he is reading my signals correctly. He'd rather be a darn gentleman than risk losing my company.

Me: "and if she wanted more?"

He turned it aside with some of his outrageous nonsense.

Brian: "Now wait. You are going too fast. If you set a raspberry pie down in front of me, I wouldn't gobble it like a hungry hound. I am a discerning person. I would nibble a little of the buttery crust. And then crush the berries up against the roof of my mouth. And then lick the sweet juices off my lips and then…"

Me: "Darn you. You make me hot just talking about food."

Brian: "Ummm, pie!"

Me: "Can't you think of something better than pie?"

Brian: "Pie ala mode?"

I will give him a pie ala mode one of theses days and he won't go back to the ones in the frozen dessert case.
Love, your hot pants sister, June

****

(via email)
   12/05/2005
Dear Hot Pants,
You'd better go sit on the ice awhile. I am calmly waiting for Mr. Right.
   Love, April

****

Thursday December 15th

Dear sister April,

Merry Christmas. I sent Dad a card and there's a little present in the mail for you. I am going to stay here and continue to sort out my life. It's almost the end of 2005. I want to spend New Years with Brian.

Brian has been letting me do some figure skating on Thursdays after the kids go home and the Zamboni is parked in its stall. The Cougars have the last ice so I have been "making a comeback." Brian is helping me with a couple of routines and we are trying to work up a benefit show for the end of the season. He doesn't want to give up his hockey skates, so about all he does is death spiral and under the legs throw. He is very strong but doesn't have the skill to get me up to an overhead carry. We achieved that position by my climbing onto his hand from the penalty box door. His hand on my pelvis was extraordinarily thrilling. My old skating partner, Alfie, used to carry me like that, but it wasn't the same. Brian's carry ended in a minor crash. We can't do that any more. One of us will get hurt. But I can still feel his big hand on my fur.

What do you think, little sister? Is it really an awakening of my sexual person? Or was it just nervous anxiety, like the fear of getting caught by our old man while our boyfriends were trying to get to second base when we would park in the driveway?

Love, June

****

(via email)
12/17/2005
Dear June,

You mean while <u>you</u> and your boyfriends were parked, and I was in the house making tea for Dad to keep him from looking out the window. You owe me. Love
    Your pure and pious sister,
    April

****

(via email)   12/17/2005
Dear Saint April, Bullwhingy!

****

December2005
    Dear Robert,

Christmas greetings and best wishes to you and Ginger. Cold and snow has finally come to Vermont, so it looks more like the yuletide season.

I borrowed a snow blower from the equipment shed and went out to my flat piece by the woods to clear the snow and build up a wall to contain the water for a skating rink. I have put down two layers with a long hose from the shed, but plan to put down more if the freezing temperatures continue. I made a fire pit and bucked up some hemlock to burn. I found an old, fake-leather couch for $100 and trucked it out to make a fine place to put on our skates. I will take June out to see it soon, though it may not be ready for skating just yet.

Brian

****

13 January 2006
Dear Robert,

I just took June back to her apartment. She spent the night here, cuddling under the down comforter with me. Sounds tame, but the action before that was quite wild. I have enjoyed her company a lot. We have good times and good talk, so I have not been at all forward, for fear of losing this lovely but married creature. I took her out in the moonlight to see my woods skating rink. On the way out, she commenced asking if I thought she was interesting. "Interesting enough for a hug if I asked for it?" A silly question already answered. "A kiss if I asked for it?" Same answer.

"More if I asked for it"?

I lit the dry hemlock that I had placed in the fire pit beforehand I pondered my answer as I watched the fire come to life and send glowing sparks into the starry sky. When I turned from my reverie, I found that June had kicked off her boots, dropped her long, wrap-around skirt, pulled off her sweater, and was just shaking the static out of her long blond hair. The warm fire-light played on her skin and on her satiny lingerie, making her seem alluringly naked. The haste of my disrobing was surely an affirmative to her question, but I clumsily fell, full face, into the snow. Laughing, she pulled me up, leaving a trail of melting snow on her bare, warm body as we reclined onto the old couch.

A gentleman does not permit himself to fantasize on the possible delights that lie within the privacy of a lady's garments. But once shown the attractive bare figure of this beautiful woman, desire rose to the occasion and the high-minded intention of prolonged adoring evaporated. I, with teen-like innocence had not believed that insane sexual desire could come upon me so quickly. I had not brought "protection." Now there are about a million hot little sperm things racing across the blue line toward the goal. And, she had taken her chemical goalie out of the net a few weeks ago, to save money. We'll have to wait and see.

As the fire died down to embers, we scooped up our clothes and ran back to my apartment for a shot of brandy

Brian

****

(via email)   01/ 25/2006
Dear foolish, lusty brother,

I see child support, alienation of affection, paternity etc. Would you like to retain my services for the next year and a half?

Robert, LLC
Ginger is blushing.

****

(via email)
    01/ 21/2006
Dear April,
I gave him pie ala mode. He liked it. There may be some unintended consequences. Love, June

****

29 January 2006
Dear brother Robert,

Just got back from taking June to Troy, New York to fulfill her father's strong request to visit. Pretty tough weekend. I think the old man liked me OK. He used to play hockey for Syracuse and we had a comfortable conversation. But he lit into June pretty heavy, reminding her that she was Catholic, and going on that nobody believes in anything anymore. "Priests want to marry or play with little boys. Married couples want to sleep around. People write books about the Virgin Mary living in Paris. The goddamn industries want to save pennies by having product made by heathens across the pond. And you, you want this fine young man instead of your good husband. Do you think Christ died on the cross for our sins? Nobody wants to think anything is sinful. Life eternal? Will your mother come back? In her wheelchair? As the radiant young beauty I married? No, Christ died because he thought that was the way to help people love each other the way He loved us. If you can't love

your husband unto death, what can you love?' June
was crying. He gave her a big hug and said, "I love
you, my daughter." And to me he said, "You are a
good man. You will find somebody." We drove
through the night to get back to Northeast Vermont. I
left June at her apartment near the college, then I drove
up to my home on the Mountain. Called her later to
make sure she was OK. I don't know how this is going
to turn out.

Brian

****

Sunday, February 5th
Dear sister June,

Dad called me and told me about the harrowing
evening he inflicted on you and your "escort." He likes
Brian well enough, but is distressed at the breach in
distance and time for you and Jon. He misses having
you around for holidays and can't understand what
conflict has arisen. "Boredom" won't satisfy his mind,
though I am empathetic to both you and Jon. I saw this
happening when you were spending so much time
trying to rise in the figure skating world. Jon just
drifted off, went to the bars and got fat; well, just a
little paunchy.

You and I are pretty women and we should
reasonably expect to be seen with men who think
highly enough of themselves, and of us, to come up to
speed in the grooming and affability departments. Jon

has fallen behind. Still, there is something to be said on behalf of the faithful dogs of the world. I was seventeen when you first brought him home and I immediately set about honing my seduction skills. No interest in sex. Just interest in affirmation. I put on my laciest bras and paraded around the house. He averted his eyes. When you and Dad got stuck in Syracuse by the snowstorm that paralyzed the northeast, Jon came and rescued me from a snowbank, drew the hot tub full and let me soak in privacy. When I came out with a towel wrapped around me, he put lotion on my back as I asked him to. He was breathing hard, but he didn't get funny with his hands. Jon and I live near each other, watch each other's Blockbuster movies, cook for each other, go to the gym together and even take an English Lit class together.

I have grown up and no longer need to practice on poor Jon, but I think am shaping him up into a pretty hunky piece of goods for someone. You?

Love, April

****

Dear April,
Friday, February 10th

You are a very persuasive little sister! I need to get away for a while to think about my life. Dad's speech has burned a little hole in my heart. I've got to see if it will heal or let me bleed to death. I wouldn't be averse to seeing the "new" Jon to find out if he is like the one I married. Can I stay with you?

Love, June

P.S. I do have to come back during the last week in March to put on the figure-skating demonstration that I promised to the Junior Hockey League.

****

Dear brother,
24 March 2006

They say, "If you love something let it go." Bad advice, I think. I let June... No, June had to go home to find herself. She went away for six weeks, during which time I was about crazy with wanting to see her. She is back now, but she didn't bring her beautiful, confident smile with her. I fear that I have lost her. We have practiced our silly little "Ice Capades" and will put it on next Thursday following the last practice. After that I don't have clue to the future except my desiring.

Brian

****

Friday 31 March
Dear Robert,

Tragedy! I tried to call you, but I guess this was the week you were taking your family to Disney World. June came back and put on a brilliant show. I did my few tricks, which the crowd loved for their clumsiness. Then June skated like an Olympic Champion. She was beautiful. Her husband had come, bringing a huge bouquet of roses, which, at the end, he held out to her with tears streaming down his face. I choked up and could barely deliver the requisite thank-you to her and to the parents. Worse: as she skated off the ice, she fell, apparently from fainting. We called the EMT's and rushed her off to the hospital. I took her husband because he was too distraught to drive and I stayed in the waiting room, while he, as next of kin, went into the ER with her. When he came out, he had a big shit-eating grin on his face and I knew what had been revealed. To my relief, the doctor came out and told me, and the concerned parents who had come along, that she was going to be OK; and nothing at all about a pregnancy. I don't know what will happen next. I called June's sister April. She will be here tomorrow morning. I'm up for the night and will drop this in the mail slot when I go back to see June.

Brian

****

2 April 2006
Dear brother Robert,

Thanks for being around when I need someone to hear my "bootless cries": June is fine, as is the fetus of undetermined age. Jon is happy that a new family has been started. June, I think, feels she has lived the pages of one of her romance novels and looks calm, even beatific. She is gone from me, of that, I am sure, but other questions may beg for answers. The little guy/gal is safe in his/her cozy Catholic womb but I am not sure about my role in his/her future. April will be here soon and I will try to hear June's desires through her.

April has, in fact arrived before the finishing of this letter. I will go on with it a bit later.

Oh my god! You should see this woman; a goddess in form-fitting cashmere! I nearly fell out of my chair. I don't know how it could be that two daughters would both be so beautiful and yet look so different. April has long, dark-brown hair flowing over her shoulders and back. She has the most lovely, wild-rose lips. And her blue eyes, set below brows that have a little extra curve, seem always to be alert and searching. I am a bit ashamed to be distracted so easily from my sorrow at losing June.

After she saw June for a time, I drove April up to the mountain and we sat in front of the big fireplace, drinking Rum and Coke and talking about the future. I confessed that June and I had a little sexual encounter shortly before she went home. April confessed that she had left two consenting adults alone in her house for an afternoon and she thought maybe... It didn't seem to her that any more confessions would be productive. "After all," she said, "medical students often donate sperm that may father children whom they are forbidden to know. Let it go." What do you think, Robert?

Brian

****

(via email)
08/04/ 2006
Dear Brian,

I agree, but that's not my lawyer answer. No fee, so you can't sue me if I have given you bad counsel.

Robert

****

Dear April,
Thursday, April 13th

Thanks for staying with me after my release from the hospital. I'm sorry that my little apartment doesn't offer more comfortable guest accommodations. I'm okay except for the normal wooziness that goes with the problem. Brian is very attentive. He drives to and from his work four days a week to make sure I don't need anything. He senses, correctly, that our relationship has changed and that his role as suitor should give way to modest friendship until I get my head on straight.

I sent Jon home to Poughkeepsie, persuading him as gently as I could that I need more time. He protested, but he went.

I feel like I am skating on a late winter pond where the ice is just breaking up. Apparently, I am about one or two months into my first trimester and uncertain about the date of conception and therefore about the baby's father. That trip home made me again see the husband I married. We had started our married life with much admiration for each other and solid plans for the hope of a home and children. That faded when my skating stressed my body and soul. I ran away to find a way to be new and joyous. I found a life as romantic as any novel. Now, though I truly love Brian, a big piece of the life that Jon and I dreamed has been put in place by willy-nilly fate. I guess I must go have a paternity test done to see what my choices are.

Love, June

****

Dear big sister,
Sunday, April 16th

Why do you feel the need to establish paternity? All that's needed here is for the baby to be loved when it arrives. Jon is thrilled. Brian would step into the role if asked. You should choose the life you want to live and disregard the idea of family line. You left the Desjardins name at the marriage altar, as will I. The child will not care what surname he or she acquires. Heritage starts anew at every birth. Don't you remember what Grammy Desjardins used to say about her mother- in-law? "Desjardins - French Garden- but there was an Irishman planting in it." You and I went to our room and laughed for an hour when we worked out the implication, of Grammy's pronouncement. Great Grandfather had married a beautiful and very social Montreal woman who apparently got around a bit. We honor a French heritage and it may be misdirected. Who cares? Il n' y a pas de quoi, and it won't make any difference to the new little kid, either

Love, April

****

(via email)
04/19/2006
Dear April,

I think that June is quite unhappy here and needs to get home to resolve some issues about her marriage. I will bring her over if you think that is a good idea. Some husbands get mean when they think they have shared a woman they love. I don't think that is true about Jon, and it certainly is not true about me. I love June and always will. We shared a brief, bright time together, which I will always cherish.

Brian

****

(via email)
04/20/06
Dear Brian,

Thank you for your kind offer to bring June. I will tell our Dad that she is coming home to cheer him up. She can stay with him. Not a word about the pregnancy. Not a word to Jon until June has made some decisions on her own. You can stay with me. I live in Newburgh, near Mount Saint Mary College, where I teach. It's a bit of drive, but the highway is fast and scenic. I'd really like to see you: we have much to discuss.

I have a one -room efficiency with guest bed/lounge off in one corner so you will have to bring your own modesty with you. You can shower and dress in the bathroom for your trip back to the mountain. April

****

(via email)
04//21/2006
Hi Robert,

I just took my lovely June to her father. She cried a lot on the way, apologizing over and over for the surging passion that has put her in such a dilemma and left me with quite a lot to contemplate. Even if she knew, she is not ready to decide which of the men whom she loves is the father. On one hand I hear the wedding liturgy; "that which God hath joined, let no man put asunder." Plus, my little aerie up on the mountain isn't a great place to raise a kid. On the other hand, I'd be a damn good dad. The little person would be skiing and playing hockey by age 3. Reading and singing, too. Shit! I'm crying now

Brian

****

(via email)
04/21/2006
Brian,

Hang in there. Ginger says you would be great dad. I concur, but she had dreamy look in her eye. I'll be glad to get you married off.

Robert

****

24 April 2006
Dear Robert,

June's sister, April, kindly invited me to stay with her when I took June back to their father. April thought it best to have a quick drop off instead of a wrenching "parting is such sweet sorrow" drama. I gladly accepted both propositions. I gratefully accepted her late night snack and crawled into the cot she made up for me. I was too washed up from the day's stresses to make much midnight conversation, so I'm afraid I didn't make a great impression.

Night closes out the worries of one day and often lets the new morning bring brighter prospects. I awoke to a vision angelic; April floating by in quite sheer sleep wear. She paused to look at the man occupying her cot, as if recollecting the previous evening. In a second or two she remembered, approved, grabbed her clothes for the day, and ducked into the bathroom, saying "snooze another fifteen minutes". I pulled the covers up and drifted contentedly, visualizing the shower occupant. She soon emerged in shorts and a scoop top short sleeve knit.

Taking a clue from her garb, I grabbed appropriate outdoor wear and stepped into the steamy bathroom. When I came out, she announced that we would be going down to the Stone Mountain Art Center which turned out to be a good place for getting better acquainted; the airplane mechanic learned that the at the mathematician recognized works by Calder and di Suvero and the math teacher was surprised that the mechanic asked to see Maya Lin's "Wavefield Storm", Goldsworthy's tree-respecting stone wall, and Lichenstein's "Mermaid", painted on a sailboat hull. I said "that looks like you." "I look like an America's cup sailboat?" she asked as she flashed her long lashes up and faked a demure smile. I want this woman, but I'm not sure I am quick enough of wit to keep up with her. As we walked between the widely scattered works we had ample time to talk about each other's values and desires. I kept to the higher ground, thinking it unseemly, in view of my dissolving relationship with June, to utter my true thoughts about her gorgeous, dark-haired sister.

We ate out at a steak house in Vales Gate and retired to April's apartment for a late-night cocktail.

In the morning I awoke to watch April, in bra and slip, drop a sky-blue silk dress over her form. She deftly zipped it up and shook out her tresses. I heard myself quoting Robert Herrick under my breath; "how sweetly flows…. the liquifaction of her clothes, " She prompted me to get going. "Special services at Mount Saint Mary today; mass and luncheon at noon, but you should be well on your way home by then." After breakfast I walked her over to campus. Lingering awhile to look down at the Hudson River, my goodbye let my passion escape and revealed more of my feelings than the "brother-in-law" kiss I intended. Composing a dozen love letters on the way home, I hardly noticed the miles slipping by.

Brian

****

25 April 2006
Dear April,

Thank you for your hospitality after I dropped off June in Troy. Your choice of the Stone Mountain Art Center as a place to broaden our friendship was truly inspired; it let me look at you without revealing how astonished I was to be with you. I am so enamored of you that I find it difficult to avoid hyperbole. Let me only say, that if Titian had seen your face he would have photo-shopped it onto his Goddess of Urbino. OK, that is a bit of hyperbole, and an anachronism to boot, but you do have a beautiful face: Ready to smile, ready to laugh, ready to be a friend. I also am ready to be a friend and, if that seems good to you, I would like to see where that might take us.

Brian Bigelow

****

Monday, May 1st, 2006
Dear Brian,
It is done! I asked Jon to go with me to the Cathedral to pray for our marriage. He is so committed, himself, that he was confused by my request and doubly confused by my tears as we knelt at the altar. This is not easy for me but it is the right thing to do. I'm not even going to go to reconciliation and confuse the priest with "it might be this or that ". Thank you for letting me go. I love you forever.

June

****

Wednesday, May 3rd
Dear big sister,
Brian stayed with me the night after he dropped you off with Dad. Just a place to stay, but I felt

electrified by his presence here. Here is a real man: Good looking, muscular, thoughtful and honest. I am weary of being hit on endlessly by graduate students. I am tired of disappointing dates with faculty men with soft hands who only think of their own gratification. I want to wear a ring and belong to someone who loves me. I want to pursue Brian, but I am hesitant because of what that may do to you and me. What do you think?

Love, April

****

Dear little sister,
Wednesday, May 10th

Brian was a part of my life that I needed to do and I am glad that I met him. Jon is a part of my life that I lost for awhile and, which now, I dearly want to hang onto. Maybe that fall on the ice knocked some perspective into my head. I am ready to follow my new found heart. You can, too.

Love, June

****

Via Teleflora
Thanks Big Sister,
    Love, little sister

****

via e-mail
05/11/2006
Dear Brian. Yes!

April

****

via e-mail
05/11/2006
Dear April,
Hurrah! I think I can bum a ride with the Air Force Reserve to Stewart. I'll give you a call to make arrangements and give you a heads up when we leave Burlington.

A very happy Brian

****

Saturday, May 21
Dear Robert,
I got a hop over to Stewart Air Base to consider a job offer. April came and picked me up to spend a couple of hours at an outside bar down by the Hudson River. I had brought along a $3 mood ring and did all the schmaltzy stuff to propose marriage. She accepted and I am really high. The mood ring went crazy with color. We'll go pick out a proper ring later. My USAF Reserve friends, alerted by cell phone, held up their flight briefly for my return hop to Vermont. Nice guys!

Brian

****

Sunday evening,
May 21ˢᵗ ,2006
Dear June,

Engaged!!! So much to attend. Brian will wrap up his work for the UPS fleet. He will take the C17 maintenance position at Stewart and may even work on Air Force One if he gets his special security clearance. He will move in with me. I will continue to work at Mount Saint Mary College, but spring is a very busy time for a math instructor trying to nudge students toward success, so we are consolidating our swift relationship by letters. His are lovely affirmations of his affection. I am very happy. He will come over next weekend to stay with me.

Love, April

****

Thursday, May 25, 2006
Dear Brian,
Congratulations! Ginger said "lucky girl." What the hell does that mean?

Robert

****

28 May 2006
Dear Robert,

I finally arranged a whole weekend with my lovely
fiancée. I finished a morning maintenance call at the
Burlington airport, showered and headed down route 7,
stopping at the Madison Brewery for dinner then
proceeding over to Albany and on down to Newburgh,
arriving at 9 o'clock. To stretch my car-cramped legs,
we went out along one of the lighted walks of the post-
exam campus. With most all of the students away, we
found it surprisingly private and romantic. The rest of
the weekend was equally enjoyable. April had a special
wish, and I granted it. What man can deny a beautiful
lady? There is more to say but I have tucked that letter
into my art book, beside Botticelli's "Birth of Venus,"
where I might find it when I am 75 and wishing to
remember young love. Brian

Dear Old Self,
Do you remember that weekend? She was so
beautiful! She had been thinking about this for a long
time. She wanted to present herself as a gift unreserved
into my hand: a loving bride to a loving groom.
Disrobing in the hall, I went into the bedroom and
found her standing by the bed, a burgundy chemise
clinging to her exquisite form. Like someone opening a
valuable present, I lifted the silky lingerie over her up-
stretched arms, letting her long brown hair cascade
down to her breasts. Our naked embrace affirmed that

we had found a safe harbor where love and patience form a breakwater against the rages of ill fortune. We soon broke from this reassuring calm and gave ourselves over to a dream of a seashore where the rhythmic tide increases its intensity until it splashes its foam upon the shore and then slowly returns to the depths from which it arose.

We shared a snifter of Bristol Cream and, feeling as peaceful as an outgoing tide, went to sleep,

We got up late the next morning, showered, took breakfast in our towels, looked adoringly at each other, then laughed and jumped back into bed for an encore. Don't you wish you could do that again?

Respectfully, Young Self.

****

via e   mail)
07/20/2006
Dear June,
 Preggers!

Love, April

****

Dear Robert,
20 July 2006

April is pregnant: due in late February. We plan to marry on August 26th in the Dominican chapel on Mount Saint Mary campus. June will be the Matron of

Honor, and I hope you will stand up with me as my
Best Man. I'm sorry to drop this on you so late. The
sequence is not quite according to Church doctrine, but
I think it's nice that the little person will be present at
our wedding. April's returning math majors are going
to be counting on their fingers trying to figure when
the "event" took place. Look for details soon. April
and I will take care of accommodations for you and
your family.

Your happy brother, Brian.
Dear June,
Friday,
August 4th, 2006

Brian and I have decided, for a number of reasons,
to marry right away. It will be a simple ceremony at
the chapel on campus, August 26th, before classes
begin. We'll have a catered reception in one of the
school's function halls, but the rest will be quite
informal. I want you to be Matron of Honor. My
former boss, old Sister Sullivan, will be smiling to see
two "good Catholic girls," obviously pregnant, up at
the altar. Brian's brother Robert will come east with
wife, Ginger, and their two boys. Robert will be Best
Man.

Love, April

****

Dear Robert,

10 September 2006

Thank you for coming to be my Best Man. For such a hasty preparation, the affair went quite well.

It was nice to see Ginger after so long a time. I suppose, now that I am "safely married," as you said, we can put away the worries that haunt your thoughts. When our old man ran off with a floozy and Mom disappeared into a bottle, Ginger came over from her own fucked-up family and took care of us. She could have been jailbait had anyone in her family given a damn. But she stayed pure. She kept her virtue for a loftier reason; she loved us both enough to not love one and lose the other. She was the Wendy to us lost boys, playing video games, helping us with our algebra, cooking, telling us which girls in school were not to get our attention. It came to a point that one of us had to leave in order for us both to grow up. The Air Force took me in to start the job. I will do damn well if I can raise a daughter as wonderful as she is.

Peace, Brian

****

(via email)
10/28/2006
Dear April,

Thank you for coming to help me bring Willow Montana into the world. She is beautiful! Jon is crazy with joy and I am so happy that I made the choices I did.

Your lovin' sister, June

****

(via email)
02/28/2007
Dear Robert and Ginger,

Celeste Avril Bigelow has arrived. Mother and daughter are fine but I am a frazzled mess.

Brian

****

Christmas 2008
Dear Dad,

Brian is off to the hillside below campus to give me a little break and give Celeste a bracing taste of cold air and a short sled ride. There's a pair of skis and a pair of skates under the Christmas tree so those activities will soon be on our agenda. I have lost some of my skill in those areas, but am ready to take them up again so I can be with my daughter and her crazy Vermont father. Music and reading are also in our lives but that comes after dark.

Brian plays hockey on a loosely organized pick-up league at West Point. Jon comes, too, and if they play on different sides it gets quite rough. Males!

We get up to Poughkeepsie about once a month to see June, Jon and Willow. The little girls get along great.

Merry Christmas!

I'll be calling you to find a good time to come up for a few days during my school break.

Love, April, Brian and Celeste

Dear Robert,

3 August 2009

Apologies for being so busy that I can't seem to get time to write. Part of that is due to a good opportunity that arose for us. Before I rejoice at some good fortune, I must express a note of sadness: The older couple downstairs that has been renting us our little apartment above the Hudson has come to the end of their ability to take care of each other. They will move to an assisted living facility in Arizona, giving us the chance to buy the whole house. April and I have both been frugal: we can meet the down payment and the qualifications for the mortgage. Good to go. My sadness is for the old couple. Bone cancer took out his knee when he was in his sixties and left his leg as a straight log. I built a ramp for him when I first moved in but other medical issues have overtaken him.

In the Song of Solomon, the bridegroom warns his bride that "the little foxes may come and eat the grapes" – a mild prediction of troubles that may befall their life. He hits way wide of the mark. Much worse can happen, as any daily newspaper will scream. I will be 60 when this mortgage is paid off and may be beginning my own decline. In the mean time, I plan to make mad passionate love to this beautiful woman as long as I can. I may stock in a truckload of celebratory Bristol Cream in anticipation of the good nights ahead.

Brian

****

1 September 2009
Dear Robert,

April is back in her classroom, telling a new batch of students that differential equations will be just as easy calculus III. (Yeah, sure!) I've taken some time off from work to make some changes in our new house. With Celeste in day care, I tore down the walls that had been built to make a separate apartment and entry for the rental. I discovered a cherry banister and balcony rail. I will rebuild the curved bottom part of the staircase that once swept into the foyer. We will retain April's tiny apartment, with its galley of mini appliances and narrow bunk, as our magical honeymoon schooner sailing high above the Hudson. Life is good!

Brian

****

Thanksgiving, 2009

Dear Robert, Ginger and boys

Sorry to miss your Thanksgiving. April's relatives clamored for us to come to Troy so they could see the little girls together. This was a command performance and the first time Jon and I brought April and June home at the same time. It's going OK, better than I expected. Our ladies prepared the meal. Jon and I will do the dishes. Jon is calling his parents, so I am taking a minute to write while I am waiting. The little girls are so close in age and appearance they could be mistaken as twins. Luckily for them, they have no perceptible traits of either Jon or me and seem to carry only the genes of the grandmother who begat the beautiful daughters we married. Their father is seated in a tiny chair while his granddaughters serve him tea at their play table. He looks as if his old blue eyes are about to flood with tears of joy. At dinner, while he was finishing a long and heartfelt grace, June looked at me across the table and silently mouthed 'Thank you". A final blessing on us all "In the Name of the Father, Son and Holy Ghost, Amen".

Happy Thanksgiving.
Your lovin' brother Brian

****

End

Spring Comes to Coppermine Brook

Subdued beneath the winter's ice and snow
The mountain stream remembers vernal strength
And murmurs threats to the rock below
Foretelling forms to be carved in time's great length.

Yet while the imprisoned water glides along
An unheard wind seeps in the valley fold,
Pushed by warm-front weather, live as song,
Mixing March air with February cold.

The forming fog sorts in deepening shades of gray
The silent shapes of lofty hardwood trees,
While, pale and blue, an ice mass falls away'
Its stony grip relinquished to the thawing breeze.

 The cracking ice portends a mighty change.
The swelling stream bursts outward toward the sea.
The glistening waters tumble from the mountain range
Shouting to the whirling seasons the joy of being free.

Mountain Flower

The lingering warm-front rain drizzles in the still air,
Waiting for the wind to shift and bring the mountain to
life once more.
Boulders teeter softly beneath the tread of climbers
Ascending to clear their minds in the wide view and
cold air.
Unlike the younger mountains on another coast
Which quake and rumble with their growth,
This old formation watches itself going down to dust
From the relentless work of lichens, roots, ice
And weather.
Here in the steep scramble of the Lion Head,
Where the last snow has drawn back beneath the
stunted trees,
And mountain ash is coming to leaf
There comes a stirring.
Forces as old as the mountain
Awaken with quickening ferocity.
Clouds pile up in the Great Gulf,
Waiting their turn in the venturi over the summit.
The wind shreds them to fractus,
Throws them down into Tuckerman ravine
Then tosses them again into towering cumulus across
the valley.
Thunder rumbles in Carter notch, beyond Wildcat.
Shadows and fog chase each other over rocky slopes.
With increasing intensity, the cold wind defends
The Alpine garden in the broad expanse, just above.
The climb hesitates for cliff dangers in the fog.

Suddenly, though, as the trail levels out, and the fog clears,
There it is:
A single diapensia sprung from its mossy foliage in a rocky crevice,
Then more and more of the tiny white flowers appear,
And pink moss campion,
And low-lying Lapland rosebay azalea,
All in a floral carpet across the Bigelow Lawn plateau.
Walking gingerly from rock to rock
So as not to spoil this splendor, the turmoil in my mind is quieted
And I am released into a new hope.
I stay awhile, listening to the wind in the ravine,
Then race the evening shadows down the eastern slope.

Notes

Mount Washington's Alpine flowers bloom briefly and abundantly about the second week of June. Several trails lead to the relatively level Alpine Garden and Bigelow lawn. The easiest starts at the parking lot near the auto toll road 6 mile post and tends south with a mild descent (The Carriage Road costs $20 for car and driver, $7 for each additional adult, $12 for motorcycle). Crossing through the Alpine Garden near the tops of the Huntington and Tuckerman's Ravines it reaches Bigelow Lawn and the Lake of the Clouds in about 2 miles.

There is a trailhead and parking at the Appalachian Mountain Club Camp in Pinkham Notch. A common path gradually ascends beside a mountain stream to the vicinity of Hermit Lake, a tarn at the mouth of Tuckerman Ravine. Although the trail goes straight into the glacial cirque and up the steep headwall, the way is likely to be blocked by snow (and skiers in bathing suits). In recent years, the Lion Head trail up onto the north shoulder has been closed due to erosion, so the most viable option is the link to the Boot Spur along the south shoulder to Bigelow Lawn, about three and half hours from the AMC trailhead.

On Mountain Washington's west side, the Base Road from Bretton Woods leads to a trailhead and parking near the Cog Railway Station. The trail starts behind and to the right of the station and ascends alongside the headwaters of the Ammonoosuc, passing spectacular waterfalls and pools, arriving at the Lake of the Clouds and Bigelow Lawn in about three hours of hiking time.

Hikers should obtain a map at the AMC camp or at the Cog Railway base station. Mountain temperatures drop about 3 degrees per thousand feet, making a cool day at the base into a freezing day at the summit so layered clothing is a wise choice. The carpet of Alpine flowers is spread across the mountain at about 5500 feet. The summit at 6288 feet can be reached in about an additional hour of hiking. Stay on the marked trails to preserve the delicate Alpine flora. Much useful information can be obtained at hikethewhites.com

Some trailhead parking now requires that a parking permit or a Golden Eagle pass be displayed in the vehicle window. These may be purchased from "vendors" (outdoor recreation stores, for example), or from the US Forest Service in Gorham New

Hampshire, or by inquiry at the Appalachian Mountain Club 603-466-2721. The cost is $3 for one day, or $20 for a full year.

The Sky Watchers

On summer days
After garden or hayfield labor
I swim a little way out into our cool lake
Turn onto my back
And float between two skies:
The one miles above, churning with condensates,
The other, a few feet below,
Ribboned with concentrates of sunlight
Refracted by the lens of restless water.
The sky above plays out its slow dynamic.
Great ships of cumulus, with sails
Gold edged in the sunlight
Leaning out of the wind,
Move majestically across the blue.
Dark shreds of cloud, torn off by the turmoil,
Scud in the wake, trying to keep up.
On other days,
As warm sea winds push across The Presidentials
And form lee waves westward over our valleys,

Parallel streets of altocumulus
Line up on the crests of cooler air.
Later in the day,
As the forms dissipate into gauzy stratus
And disappear,
The swifts and swallows come
To fly in the brief, white sky.

As a youth, he may have learned to swim,
But he thought less about water as recreation
Than as harbor, opening out into the sea.
He went from his home to nearby Bremerhaven
To board a tramp steamer bound for Peking.
As a deck hand he became one with the elements.
And this experience stayed with him.
When he later came ashore to stay.
He watched the sky all the time and when he could
He painted.

Most often, he hitched his clouds to the horizon:
To the earthbound features that shape the weather
Or record its unrelenting impact.
His prodigious watercolor brush captured
The weather's interaction with the land:
Valley fog drawn toward sun-warmed summits,
And clouds boiling up out of craggy ravines,
And wisps of cloud rolling down into glacial valleys,
And sleety snow obliterating pasture fence-lines.
Sometimes, though,
He found interesting events happening directly
overhead
Where the dark bases of cumulonimbus

With undulating mammae and streaking virga,
Contrast with the stark white above.
When he anticipated such powerful weather,
He brought along a thick slab of black glass
And laid it on the ground to view the mirrored sky.
The heavens fell to earth in true but muted tones,
Giving an illusion of a window into an inner earth
Where trees like ours pointed inward,
And the border of grasses grew upward and downward
From roots in a paper-thin, crust of soil.
Leaning over to view the sky and his antipodean self
He scoffed, "They will look at these pictures
And ask if they are surreal art."
One February day, too cold for painting,
We went onto Cannon Mountain to study ice feathers
Blown onto exposed structures,
Reaching out into the wind that formed them.
We wandered among snow-crusted firs
With tops that bent down at us
Like threatening polar bears.
He laughed and put up his arms in mock defense.
Now, in Aviano,
I watch a snow squall
Moving swiftly along Italy's northern border,
Dusting staggered shelves of rock
Thrust up from an ancient sea.
Behind them, the Alps
We had planned to climb.

On Moosilauke Without You

On Moosilauke without you
I search for a trail which in the deep of winter
Led us over an icy shoulder
To a line of stunted firs that halted our ascent.

Somewhere under the southern peak
A faltering path rises out of the Carriage Road,
Crests on a rounded pavement,
And dives toward a forest on the western slope.

Under the summer sun
No sign of such a path appears.
No wearing of the mossy floor,
Not even a parting in the hardwood forest
Where we set out with skis and poles
To climb.

Yet, memory recalls the place
As clearly as it recalls your laughter
Ringing the crystal air
When you found rescue for your icy hands
Under my woolen shirt.
Puzzling over map and compass
We huddled in a small ravine
Listening to the wind scream overhead
And studying the unbroken line of trees ahead.
In fun you said Old Benton,
Learning from the Baba Yaga,
Threw down a hairbrush and an incantation,
Making forests grow

Where none had grown before.

Ways are lost, though,
Without the work of wizardry.
Division imposed itself upon the wishes of the heart
We had shouted to each other
Above the howling wind in the ravine
And when we went from there
We were alone
Without map or compass
To guide us back.

This dark mountain
With its hairbrush forests and lost ravines
Invites belief in magic.
So I've returned,
Hoping to find that glaciered rock
And hear your laughter
Chiding my sad face
And uncertain steps
Before the night comes.

Kevin O'Connor's St. Patrick's Day Surprise

This play moves its plot with the help of magic.
Nobody believes in magic,
of course, so a little suspended disbelief may be
required. Whether or not the ethereal players are real is
of little importance. What matters is the receptiveness
of the earthly characters, as possibilities, magic or
otherwise, are presented. Magic happens all the time; a
kind word, a thoughtful gesture, a hug can make
beautiful changes if accepted by a prepared heart.

The Scene: Forward, stage right, a recreational vehicle,
sliced lengthwise shows the interior of Kevin's living
space. Table, chairs, appliances, and a closet complete
a comfortable but compact living arrangement. The
back of the vehicle has a bathroom (not shown), a bed,
and a shower area with translucent glass around the
stall. At the front of the vehicle, the living space
extends over the driver/passenger compartment,
providing a cozy sleeping area with windows front and
side. The vehicle right side wall has a door and a large
picture window. Household equipment and drawers fit
tightly into cabinets below the window.

Visible behind the RV and more center stage, the
framework and roof of an incomplete house provide a
second stage in the form of the exposed second floor.
A stairway leads up to it.

Painted scenery implies that a road passes behind the house and over a hill. Out-sized direction signs point to "Bradford," right stage and "W. Fairlee," left stage. A driveway leads from the road around the left end of the house and into the space between the house and RV. The space will conceal a subcompact car that can be pulled out into the visible area as needed. The coming and going of Kevin's truck will be achieved by a projection on the driveway space or by a removable flat image.

Painted and fake trees give an illusion of thick woods. A clear area becomes the projection screen for the moose that appears and disappears, as if by magic.

A scraggly tree on the far left stage completes the scene. A projection screen, on which Father John shows his photos, can be lowered to completely conceal the tree.
True perspective of what could or could not be seen from inside the RV must be disregarded. It's just another part of the magic and suspended disbelief. Likewise, the passage of time must be implied by briefly dimming the stage lights.

A stage manager may offer comments from time to time.

 Father John Frere, dressed in black shirt, clerical collar and raveled sweater, enters and sits down at a chair by the table.

Kevin O'Connor [looking up from his book, in mock sarcasm]
Make yourself comfortable.

F.J.   What? I'm going to break in here and steal your frypan? I'm a priest. I can be trusted and I saw you were reading and I know how I hate to be disturbed in the middle of a paragraph.

K. [Pouring tea for his guest.]
Thanks. You are always welcome, whether you knock or not. What brings you out tonight?

F.J.   I brought over some slides of the photos I took last week when you drove me over to Cabot. That was a strange day. A beautiful day with cowslips coming bright yellow in the spring-wet meadow and poplars coming dusty green into leaf. But you were at a low point, bewailing your upcoming forty-third birthday and complaining that there were no new leaves – no new opportunities emerging for you.

K   I guess that's right. Everything about spring makes a person want to be in love but that part of my life is pretty much over. I had been thinking about that clip of Eduard Muybridge you had shown me some weeks before. After his successful pre-cinema series of the running horse, he made a self-despising series of his old self lumbering along naked, documenting his lost youth. I'm sorry if I injected some gloom on the day.

F.J.   Well, it turned out to be quite funny. You spotted an old lightning-struck tree out in a hayfield that looked as if spring would bring it few leaves, or none. Seeing a metaphor for your own life's declining promise, you stopped and instructed me to get set with the cameras while you ran out behind the tree's big trunk. Next thing I knew your were standing beside it without a stitch of clothes on. I could hear a car coming up the road. Fastest photo-shoot I've ever done. Got it on both cameras.

K.   I ducked behind the tree just in time. Then we got to laughing like two bad boys who didn't get caught. I felt quite cheered by my naughtiness.

F.J. [turning on the projector as a screen rolls down in front of the tree on the far left stage.] Well here they are. First the color slide:…Here you are full frontal and in glorious color. And now the Plus X black and white made into a slide. [pauses to explain] The Plus X has sensitivities beyond the range of the human eye."

K.   My God! There's a child up in the tree – a little girl in some kind of costume, looking down at me with my ass hanging out. How come you didn't see her?

F.J.   She wasn't there when I took the picture.

K.   You photo-shopped her in?

F.J.   I am a priest. I don't lie. I don't have a camera that lies. She has to be a being that has form only in the

UV range. Some sort of magical spirit. I don't have another explanation.

K.   You want to say leprechaun, don't you? A Saint Patrick's Day visitor.

F.J.   Well…

K.   John, look out the window.
[The image of a moose, or rather more of a Bullwinkle caricature of a moose, is projected onto the space visible out the RV window.]

F.J.   A moose! A big beautiful moose! God bless you, magnificent creature.

K.   Don't bless that moose. I'm going to kill that moose and put three years of steaks down in my freezer. Problem is, he comes and goes like that girl in the tree. Every year he writes to the Fish and Game Department to see if I have obtained a moose permit in the lottery. If I have, he goes off to Victory Bog or Canada. If not, he hangs around and looks in my window and grins.

F.J.   A grinning moose? With good penmanship and postage stamps? That's a bit of a hyperbole, isn't it? I get your point, but I can see the moose. The girl in the tree is some kind of spirit, telling you to be receptive to magic, even if it's the ordinary kind that comes in kind words or a call for help.

[The moose image fades.]

K. 	Be that as it may. A lot of unexplained events occur around Old Buffalo Mountain. I'm getting used to it. I'm not about to take it as any kind of omen or sign that I should change my ways. I'll still be a sullen old bachelor next time you see me.

F.J. [Packing up his equipment. As the screen rolls up, a girl in an Irish dance costume climbs down from the tree and dances off into the woods.]
Then how about next week. Opening day. We can try our luck on the upper Waits River.

K. 	Give me a call. Do you need a ride home?

F. J. 	No, thanks. Plenty of moonlight to show me the way. Good night.
[Father John exits. Stage lights dim. Kevin turns out his light.]

[Spot light on the stage manager.}

Mgr. When I produced "the Student Prince" in Munich, I was able to have a carriage and a four-hand team of horses drive across the stage. Our humble stage will not support the passage of horse or carriage or automobile. We'll supply cardboard cut-outs, some auto noises and headlight glare. The rest is up to you. Suspended disbelief, you know. I hear a car coming now.

[Spot light fades. Lights appear coming along the Bradford Road, accompanied by the clatter of an engine in poor health. Security lights come on above Kevin's driveway to reveal a sub-compact car emitting clouds of steam. A woman (Beryl) is kicking it savagely.]

Beryl Fuckin' shitbag bastard" [another kick] fuckin' shitbag bastard [a fist onto the hood] "fuckin' shitbag bastard.

[Lights on in the RV. Kevin emerges, attired in a red plaid hunting jacket, hairy legs sticking out under.]

K. umm, can I help you?

B. The bastard beat me up and then shot a hole in my radiator because he "loved me too much" to let me leave. What an asshole!

K. "Let me see your face."

B. [Perceiving at last some safety turns to him and lets go a torrent of tears.]

K. Jesus! Your forehead is bleeding and your eyes are going to be swollen shut. You've got to get a cold pack right away. Come inside.
[They go inside the RV. Kevin applies a bandage and prepares an ice pack, which he holds gently on her brow.]

B.   I was trying to get to my cousin's home in Barre but my vision got blurry and I pulled off Route 25 onto a side road and got lost. The bastard slammed me with an empty bottle and blood from the cut kept getting in my eyes.

K.   Your car is fried. I'll take you there in the morning, if you want.

B.   I'll sleep in my car and wait.

K.   No, no. It's too cold for that. I won't hear of it. You can have my bed. The sheets aren't bad for a bachelor guy. I'll grab my sleeping bag and roll it out under the stars. You can lock me out if you are uneasy.

B.   I'm not afraid.

[Kevin goes outside, rolls out the sleeping bag. Beryl turns down the bed covers. Lights fade. Spotlight on the sprite dancing briefly on the upper deck of the house. Off briefly. Lights of a sunrise hue slowly come to reveal Kevin busy at the stove and Beryl comfortably in bed, hugging a pillow. She awakes.]

B.   Bed *and* breakfast?

K.   Sure, even for slug-a-beds who rise after 7 o'clock.

B.   Actually, I awoke about dawn. A little girl in a fancy costume looked in my window, then ran off into the woods.

K.   Neighbor's kid. You look a little better this morning and I think your eye will be OK. We didn't make introductions last night. I'm Kevin. Do you want to tell me about yourself?

B.   Beryl. b-e-r-y-l

K.   Beryl is New Hampshire's state mineral. You are perhaps from New Hampshire?

B.   Manchester, originally, until I moved to White River to live with that drunken S.O.B. who beat me up every Saturday.

K.   Well, now you are stuck on a hill between Bradford and Fairlee, and your car is cooked. We'll check it out after breakfast to see how bad it is, but I am sure it's not going anywhere for awhile. Do you want me to drive you to Barre?

B.   Could I stay here for a few days, maybe get my car repaired and get the hell out of New England and go somewhere he can't get at me. If I go to my cousin's, he'll come and get me in a day or two. He's done it before and he will be more pissed than ever.

K.   I recycle my bottles by using them for target practice up at the end of my drive. I doubt he will come closer when he sees that and realizes he has passed into rifle range. Have another cup of coffee, while I check out your rig. I'll run the hose out and fill the radiator. If the engine will turn over the prognosis will be more optimistic.

[He goes to the car. After a long cranking, the engine starts and plumes of white smoke appear from the exhaust. Kevin returns.]

K.   Half good. The pistons haven't seized but the head gasket is blown and the head is probably warped. A week. You can stay a week and help me bring your car back to life. As a mechanic, I specialize in diesels. Some
company is sure to call me in, so work here may go a little slower. I'll make up the bed fresh for you, and I'll camp in the framework out back.

B.   While you were outside, I explored your RV and found the cozy nook over the cab. I don't want to push you out of your area, and I dream about being tucked away in a safe place, like a baby. Please?

K.   OK, I guess. We can manage the privacy issue. It would be nice to have some company for a change. [The sprite dances across the stage] Now let's see what we can do about that carcass in the driveway. I've laid out some of my uniforms from my old job at the Chevy garage. They'll be a little loose but they will spare your clothes. Come join me and learn a new trade.

[He goes outside, Beryl strips to underthings, dons the comically large shirt and pants and joins Kevin looking into the engine compartment. Tool sounds. Actors freeze in a working pose. The light dims and the stage manager steps into the spotlight. The sprite dances across the stage.]

Stage Manager Kevin and Beryl are now roommates and you might be expecting some salacious activity. But all we can offer is lot of tool sounds and an occasional cuss word as the work progresses. So we will skip over all that and bring you to the morning of the fifth day.
[As sunlight spills onto the scenery. Kevin enters, buttoning his shirt and speaking up to Beryl in her nest.]

K.   I've got to check out a big generator over in Hanover. I'm going to grab breakfast at the diner. I'll be gone until late in the day, so help yourself to the refrigerator or the bookshelf. Or you can sleep in if you prefer.

[Beryl peeks out.]
B.   I'll do dishes and tidy up the clutter. Do you mind if I throw my clothes in the washer while you're away?
K. Not at all. See you tonight

[The image of Kevin's car fades and the sound indicates he is driving toward West Fairlee. Beryl arises, and emerges dressed, arranges magazines,

washes dishes, reads, sweeps, looks out the window,
etc. Stage lights shift from left to right , alluding to the
passage of time until about 4 pm. She undresses,
throws all her duds into the washer and steps into the
shower. Stepping out, she wraps up in a towel, just as
Father John enters and sits down uninvited in his usual
place at the table.]

B.   Kevin?

[Father John jumps up at the sound of a woman's
voice.]

F. J.   Kevin?

B.   Obviously not. Who are you?

F. J.   I'm John. I'm a priest.

B.   You also appear to be a man. You may have
noticed that I am a woman.

F. J.   I noticed. I mean I…

B.   Perhaps you wouldn't mind sitting outside by
the door while we sort out who we are. I will find
something to wear.

[Father John goes outside and sits on the front bumper
of the RV. Beryl dons Kevin's red plaid hunting jacket.
Its length comes to mid thigh to make a comical but
alluring miniskirt.]

B.   Now then, you may come in. I was here first so you tell me who you are.

[Father John enters]

F. J.   I'm a friend of Kevin's. I am a photographer.

B. [Coyly opens the collar just a little.] Maybe I shouldn't have put on this great big coat.

F. J.   No, no. I do nature photography.

B.   "Under this coat I am about as natural as can be."

F. J. [Heavenward]   Oh God, why are you always making me regret my vows of celibacy?

B.   OK, fair is fair and I will tell you about myself: I found Kevin by some lucky and mysterious circumstances. His kindness has helped me get a better grip on my life. My hope had been trampled by an abusive jerk who thought he owned me and I was about to cross over a very dark edge. Kevin is letting me stay in that cubby up over the cab while he repairs my car. I am trying to keep from being a burden but I am clinging to this rock of a man like a shipwrecked seaman. Sorry to scare you. I'm a bit of a nut case."

F.J.   Oh daughter! God loves you. Be strong. I hear your clothes dryer beeping. I'll go. I won't impugn your virtue but I am going to give Kevin quite a lot of ribbing about this."

[He leaves, striding up the road with his walking stick.]

[The projection of Kevin's truck in the driveway indicates that he has returned. Beryl has made dinner seen on the table. He enters, washes up and sits down with her.]

K.   This is nice. You have been spoiling me with home cooked meals all week. How will I ever be able to go back to Banquet frozen dinners after you leave?

B.   I met your friend, Father John, today. He walked in and sat down as if he owned the place.

K.   Always does. We've been hopeless old bachelors for so long we have forgotten how to act like civilized people. Did he scare you?

B.   No, just surprised me. I was stepping out of the shower. He thought I was you.

K.   He hasn't been a priest for *that* long. I'll razz him for disturbing a lady's bath. I'm sorry I wasn't here to enjoy his embarrassment.

B.   Kevin, do you ever see dancers up on the second floor of the house? I think I see them – young girls in fancy costumes, dancing to jigs and other Irish music. I think I can hear it, but maybe my imagination is filling it in.

K.　　These woods have a lot of strange events going on, like my disappearing moose, but I believe spirits or ghosts appear as shadows of things that once happened. There was once a hope in the house that there would be dancing and music, but I dashed it to pieces. Nothing was left out of which hope, or love or ghosts might evolve. The sprites are just your imagination taking over. Think of it as entertainment and be happy.

B.　　Kevin, maybe it is a sign of something wonderful about to happen, like spring being announced by the arrival of robins or by the songs of peepers down in the swamp.

K.　　Beryl, you are 23. I am 43. Something has happened to my hope in those extra 20 years and I'm not sure I can reverse it. Call it "getting old".

B.　　Kevin, you are not old! You are as strong as any athlete and better looking than most. More importantly, you are genuinely nice. And smart, too. I feel very secure when I am with you, and I haven't felt that for a long time.

K.　　Sorry to be putting out negative vibes. It's because this repair job is almost done and you will be scooting out of here for California.

B.   Will not.

K.   What?

B.   I found a waitress job down in Bradford, in your newspaper. I called my old boss and asked him to phone in a recommendation. They hired me sight unseen. I'm good! Maybe you will let me stay here.

K.   Then you will need your car sooner. There's still a little daylight left. Let's go out and pull that radiator out. Last task. We'll have to get it soldered or find a replacement in the junkyard. And yes, you can stay.

[They go out. Kevin lifts the radiator out. Beryl gives a startled gasp.]

 K.   Are you alright? You look as if you have seen a ghost.

B.   That hole could have been a hole in me!

Light fades. Stage manager steps into the spotlight.

Stage Manager.   This play has slipped into a kind of static condition. Kevin is working almost every day, and Beryl is working at the restaurant until closing. They come home and crawl into their separate corners of the RV. Kevin puts fresh wildflowers on the table. Beryl brings home treats from the restaurant. Kind of like an old married couple. I can't interpret their thoughts for you. Let's look in on them after two more weeks. Calm seas sometimes have strong undercurrents.

[Stage lights come up to find Kevin and Father John just returning from a day of fishing, putting away tackle and opening bottles of beer.]

F. J.   What was wrong with you out there today? The fish would rise to your fly, and you were daydreaming too much to set the hook.

K.   I'm considering where to take my relationship with Beryl. I would like to have us be more than room mates, but I feel weighed down by past events – past mistakes. I function well day to day. I have friends. I do good things for people. But I was a jerk once and I may still be one. Did you ever hear confession with a beer in your hand?

F. J.   I'll tell you a secret of the clergy. We don't listen very acutely in the confessional. God listens."

K.   I need to do this. You will understand. Father forgive me for I have sinned. (Isn't that the way it starts?) You already know, of course, because you saw the newly-weds sawing and nailing to put together the bones of the house. Maybe you also have the power to see a bank account slowly growing to push the project to completion. I'm sure you know what Carly saw when she came home and found me consummating an old lust with a pretty woman who had been under my supervision in my transportation unit in Dessert Storm. Army rules required an arms-length admiration. But when Ellen got out and had some anxieties about her up-coming marriage she came to me for reassurance. What I gave her instead was unforgivable. Carly, understandably, did not forgive me. She emptied out our bank account and took off. My self-imposed penance of poverty and celibacy hasn't done a thing to relieve my misery. Now, another person – a beautiful fragile person - has come into my life seeking reassurance. God, help me to do what's right.

F. J.   You are forgiven, my son. (That's the standard ending but I believe it with all my heart.) Go and sin no more.

[Kevin wipes away a tear.]

K.   You have always said that I would feel better if I got rid of old baggage. I seem lighter, even a bit giddy. Would you like another beer?

F.J.   No thanks, I've got to be on my way. And I hear Beryl's car coming up the Bradford Road.

[Beryl enters, plunks herself down at the table and starts drinking Kevin's beer.]

B.   Bad night. Busload of poor tippers crowding out the regulars. Fussy! Making me feel like the nobody I have always been.

Kevin, I don't want to be Beryl any more. My parents
named me lovingly but I was a barrel my first
seventeen years of life and kids at school just piled it
on. In my senior year, the coaches took pity on me and
pushed me into sports.   Soccer, dance
and then track. I wasn't any good of course, but the
pounds melted away and I was left with a fairly lean
body except for these boobs. I got noticed. I got invited
to the senior prom. I bought a beautiful dress. I was
going to be pretty. But he didn't want to go to the prom
and dance with me. He took me out to the lake and
fucked me. I didn't have the self esteem to say "no".
You said, when we first met, that I was a gem. I don't
want to be a barrel or a Beryl any longer. I don't want
to be who I was. I want to be beautiful."

K.   "You *are* beautiful. Furthermore, when clear
beryl takes up a bit of chromium during its formation,
it becomes a vivid green gem stone. To me, you are
that loveliest of gems. I proclaim you "Emerald.""

[They hold hands. Lights fade. Stage manager steps
into the spotlight.}

Stage Manager.   You may be expecting the rapid
fruition of this relationship, but the road to true love is
never smooth, as you may have heard. Carly, Kevin's
ex-wife, has stopped briefly but must return to
Burlington for a flight. She left a letter for Kevin."

[Father John walks up to the door of the RV, knocks
lightly and starts to let himself in. Emerald is sitting on

the second floor of the house with her legs dangling over. She calls to Father John, who has not noticed her.]

E.   Father John, up here. Come up and sit with me. Use the stairway but be careful."

[F.J. ascends, sits by Emerald, embraces her with one arm.]

F.J.   "Hey, why so woeful? You are too tough to cry, but you've been crying."

E. On certain nights when I look up here from the window in my cubby I imagine that I see dancers. I thought Kevin and I might go dancing here someday, but now an apparition from his past has come to cloud this happy vision. Carly came back today. She wept to see the house so unfinished and forlorn after twenty years. I felt bad but I couldn't help comparing myself to her. She is an elegant lady - tall, with long blond hair and a beautiful dress. She is older but still classic like a sports car. I am a dump truck with big bumpers, a sturdy girl who can hoist a tray of five entrees, or cushion half a dozen mugs of beer against my chest. All I need is a butterfly tattoo on my butt to certify my low class, high-school-educated, going-nowhere life. Kevin has had the best. How could he ever want me? I tried to go back to Bradford and find a room, but the damned moose blocked my way. Then I tried to go the other direction to West Fairlee, and there he was again. I love Kevin and I don't give a damn about the twenty years that worry him. I fear that the letter she left for him will awaken a love that should be for me but which seems to be stalled at the starting line. He is just stuck with me.

[The moose appears briefly in a clearing by the house.]

F. J.   You are not interpreting Kevin correctly. He dearly wants to scoop you up and hold you. But Kevin is an old deer hunter and he knows that the quarry can sense intentions even with the slightest motion. Flash of white tail and it's gone into the underbrush. He is afraid that if he spoke his affection, you might think he is putting the moves on, and you would run. He loves you but he has no idea how to proceed.

E   He has picked up his grooming since I moved in. He shaves and puts on a nice aftershave. He changes his shirt for dinner. He always looks nice. Those are better signs of respect than I have had from anyone in forever. Yet, I don't see any sign that he wants the relationship to go further.
I'll let you go and just crawl into my cubby. Good night, Father John."

F. J.   Good night, Emerald. I will say something more secular than you might expect of me: You are beautiful!

[Lights fade briefly. Lights on. Kevin and Father John are seated at the table, beer in hand.]

K.   Hey, Thanks for coming over, Carly came by to return my portion of the house money and to ask my forgiveness for her reluctance to hear my pleas so many years ago. The money is nice. The better consolation lies in my learning that she married, had two boys, made a fortune investing her portion of the house money and found happiness.

F. J.   But she spooked Emerald.

K.   I know. Everything in Emerald's life has conspired to make her feel unsure. I think she now feels secure but I am baffled as to how to make her feel loved. I could do a Romeo and Juliet scene up to her in her cubby above the RV cab. Pretty lame!

F. J.   Right.

K.   John, I'm a romantic at heart. I had read *Cyrano de Bergerac* five times before I had my first date. I was ready to make some woman feel like a princess. Then I screwed up. Twice. You need to help me to keep this one chance on track.

F. J.   I also was a romantic. I love women! You know that I was professional photographer before I was a priest, but what I never told you is that I was a fashion photographer, taking pictures of gorgeoous women in pretty dresses for glossy magazines. I love women in the abstract but I never could warm up to courting any one of them. Too many choices, I like to tell myself. Really, though, the hook was already in me from my family's expectations, from my own expectations. When you were reading *Cyrano*, I was reading *The Keys of the Kingdom*. Anyway I know a thing or two about making a woman feel beautiful."

K.   And that is?

F. J.   Put her in a pretty dress and take her picture.

K.   Simple as that, you think? How does that translate into her recognition that *I* admire her.

F. J.   Here's my plan: I know the ladies at a high-class boutique down in Hanover. They will let me do anything I ask. I'll ask Emerald to pose in various outfits that she and the sales ladies like, supposedly for advertisements. Then I'll secretly have the clerk set aside the one most flattering, and you can go down and buy it for her. It'll fit. She will love it. You will be the hero who mysteriously knows what she likes.

K.   You are too much of this world to be a priest; I don't know why the diocese keeps you. Let's do it.

[Lights dim briefly. The sprite dances across the stage]

The Stage Manager appears in the spotlight.

Stage Manager   The plan has taken shape. Kevin has picked up the pretty dress that Emerald liked, and stopped at the jewelry store next door. He has returned in the early evening as stars appear above the stage.

Emerald is sitting on the second floor with legs dangling over the edge. Kevin arrives on the lawn below and speaks up to her.

K.　　Aha! A brighter star than I have ever seen before now shines in my heaven. I will consult my almanac: It says that a supernova of love is bursting tonight in the vicinity of Old Buffalo Mountain. Venus reigns in my constellation of Pisces and has broken the bonds of indecision. Shall I come up?

E.　　I'll be afraid, you amorous old woodchuck. What's in that package?

K.　　Oh, it's nothing. I bought it thinking that I could make someone who is radiantly beautiful even more lovely. I think that is folly. I will take it back to the store.

E.　　You move an inch toward your truck and I will drop a board on your head. Did you really bring me something nice?

K.　　Look for yourself. Here, catch.

[Emerald looks in the box…]

E.　　Oh!

[She moves back into the shadows, stripping to lingerie and tossing the garments over the side. She reappears in front in an elegant summer dress, white with bold flower design.]

K.　　How about a little night music?

[He goes to the truck and turns on a CD player.]

K.　　Now?

E.　　Yes.

[He goes up. They dance, gradually going from a Texas two-step to a waltz as the music changes. The music ends.]

K.　　I'll put on another CD.

[He goes to the truck. Romantic music is heard. He goes near the bottom of the stage and speaks up to Emerald.]

K.　　I almost forgot. I have another present. Would you like to see?

E.　　Oh?

[Kevin opens the box. A shaft of green light shoots up.]

E.　　Is that…? Is that…? An emerald ? An engagement ring?

K.　　Yes.

E.　　Oh Kevin. Say the words! Say the words!

J.　　Beautiful, Emerald, will you marry me?

E.　　Come up here, you marvelous man!

[Kevin ascends. They embrace. The sprite dances across the stage. Father John appears, coming along the road from his house.]

F. J.　　What's all the ruckus. I could hear the music all the way over to my place.

E.　　Oh John, come up here and marry us.

F. J.　　I don't think the bishop would approve. How about a short version, with the proviso that you promise to show up in church for the real thing. OK. Hold hands. Kevin, do you take this woman?

K.　　I do.

F. J.　　Emerald, do you take this man?

E.　　I do,

F. J.   I proclaim you consenting adults and best of friends. I'm going home and finish my sleep. I expect to be invited to a party next week.

[He leaves. Lights fade. The Stage master appears in the spotlight.]

Stage Manager.   There is a bedroom scene. You may place it in time according to your imagination or your sense of propriety. I will tell you that later on there will come a little girl who will learn to bait her own fishhook, hunt deer and field dress the carcass. Let's look in. The bed covers will protect our eyes from too much information."

E.   Kevin, you are so nervous you are shaking. Relax. Come here. Closer. There, gotcha. How do you like that?

K.   Mmf.

E.   Relax. Breathe. Stop resisting. That's a little better.

K.   Mmmf

E.   Are you laughing?

K.   [In muffled tones] Your girlfriend is pretty big up front. [Kevin is laughing]

E.   Emerald stops him. Wait, We'll tell this together. [Both laughing]

E. and K.   [In mock male voice, with Kevin, struggling to join in. Both laughing.] Your girlfriend is pretty big up front. Does she wear a C cup or a D cup?

E.   Stop laughing before we get to the punch line. [Kevin is laughing] [Continuing in fake male voice] Neither, She wears a ten and a half.
C'mon Kevin, you can do this.

E.   [In more male voice than before] What does she use to measure with?

K.   [Managing to chime in before collapsing into unfettered merriment] A Stetson. [More laughter] Oh god Emerald, I haven't laughed in 20 years. Hold me. I am about to become a blubbering old fool.

E.   Turn out the light.

Sprites come out of the woods and dance across the stage

                              Fini
Emerald and Kevin appear for bows, dressed in hunting jackets with bare legs below.

    Dedicated to the memory of Father John Bruder, A friend to everyone in the Northeast Kingdom of Vermont.

A Summer Pig

As the land first appears from under its long burden of snow, it brings on an impatience to see things growing once more. For some folks, that impatience turns toward planning for a garden. For others, animal husbandry beckons. Chicks and lambs and even dairy replacement calves can lure the otherwise sensible person into small-time agriculture.

Not to be overlooked in this hierarchy of choices comes the summer pig. Not as cuddly as bunnies or ducklings, a baby pig lined up with its suckling siblings on the contented sow has a unique attractiveness. Homer Johnson, a fellow employee where I worked, kept hogs for breeding. He convinced me that a small investment in the spring would yield a good return in the fall, so I went to visit his small barn in Lyndonville where several farrowing pens kept individual sows and their offspring. In each pen, a grating with piglet-wide spacing allowed escape to an adjacent space as a precaution against accidental crushing by the sow. Weaned pigs from an earlier litter were for sale in another pen so a little shoat came home with us in a cardboard box to his Joes Brook home.

We kept him in our barn for a time, feeding him on a grain-store mix. The vet came and made some necessary changes because the meat of an ungelded male would have a less desirable taste. As warmer weather came, the pig was given a pig house with a burlap door in an electric fenced area behind the house.

The thought was that the he would root out weeds in what might become next year's garden. That didn't take long. A pig's nose has the digging power of an army entrenching tool. In fact, a clothier of the early 20th century bragged "Fincks Work Garments: Wear like a Pig's Nose". The idea was soon revealed to be less clever than planned: In the clay soil laid down in some ancient lake bed, the pigs narrow hooves were like spike heels on a hefty lady; The proposed garden plot became solid as airport tarmac.

Pigs are smart. Ours soon learned to short out the electric fence by pushing his feeding trough up against the wire and then escaping to root in nearby gardens. Enticed to return for supper each time, this game went on until a knock-down, high voltage fencer was purchased.

Pigs are also companiable. One family up in the county brought theirs home and let it stay in the house but soon learned that there are no doors that can convince a housebroken 200 pound hog that it should live outside in the cold. Although most pig husbands don't keep their animals as pets, there is some satisfaction in talking to an appreciative and attentive pig that is enjoying a few scratches behind the ears. There is a story - perhaps only the product of a mischievous imagination and a long winter- about an old bachelor in our county who enjoyed talking to his pigs but found that his pigs' attention spans were shorter than the topic of conversation. He began interspersing his talk with whistling to keep them focused on what he had to say. According to the

legend, he even kept this habit when he came to town to buy groceries.

A summer pig changes garden vegetables, like excess zucchini and raccoon damaged corn, into pork chops. To express appreciation for this marvelous transformation most owners name their pigs in a way that let's them know how much they are valued. Names like "pork chops" come to mind ("filet de porc aux pruneaux" or other gourmet names might be too long). We gave our pigs more general names such as "Copious" or "Bountiful". One summer, however, our pig seemed especially to enjoy lounging in his muddy pen. We named that one "Primary Standard" and invited our friends to come and see if they were happier or less happy than a pig in wallow.

My grandparents raised pigs on this same farm. The wooden sty dissolved long ago, but some of the seeds in the last apples thrown into the pen germinated and grew into a too-dense orchard with fruit suitable only for the few deer that venture close to the farmstead. In addition to the apples and garden leftovers, these pigs grew fat on skim milk. The main saleable product of this eight jersey farm was rich creamy milk to be made into butter. An important step in this manufacture was accomplished by the Delaval Separator, an ingenious centrifuge device of enclosed, spinning, stacked cones that sent the more dense skim milk out to one spout while the cream floated out another spout. Cranked by hand, this device required no more power than a standard ten year-old boy. The skim milk would have been a waste product but it was fed, with a bit of grain, to the pigs. "Slopping the pigs" was certainly the correct phrase for the emptying a bucket of this mixture into the trough. At times there was an excess of skim milk and it was poured into a wooden barrel near the separator, where it gradually formed into a cottage cheese that floated to the top. This also became part of the porkers diet. Always covered with flies, it was not an attractive delicacy.

The pigs had started their life in the barn very early in the spring. Two or three were selected and the other shoats were sold. When the fall weather became reliably cold, each massive hog was roped on a hind leg and led up to the main floor of the barn where a barrel of water steamed menacingly. I never saw the next step because my grandmother took me on a walk up the road. But I heard it! When we returned the slaughtered hog, stuck and bled, was hanging by a hind leg chained to a block and tackle on a beam above the hot water and the men were standing on the bloody floor scraping bristles.

The meat was preserved by smoking the hams, making and canning mincemeat, preparing sausage, putting the strips of pork fat down into large crocks with layers of salt where they became salt pork. Much of the remaining fatback was "tried out" by heating in a kettle on the wood stove to form the melt that would become lard for all the baking and frying needs of the farm kitchen. A crispy and delicious by-product called cracklins was spread out on brown paper bags to drain and cool before being sprinkled with salt and consumed.

Some time in the fall, before deer season, our own summer pig chores had to come to an end. An appointment was made. The fairly cooperative animal was coaxed into a borrowed, slatted crate and for the second and last time taken for a ride. Ever calm and expert at his work, charcutier "Bub" Dresser dispatched the unsuspecting animal and soon dispersed the carcass to ham smokers, sausage makers and others, who returned the meat in labeled and wrapped white packages conveniently sized for a home freezer.

We comforted ourselves in the loss of our twice-a-day social exchange by remembering that the patient listener had lived a summer life, free of stinging sleet and bone chilling cold. He might even be reincarnated in the next year's summer pig.

Of course a summer pig is not for everyone. As with any animal, except those out to pasture, feeding is required morning and evening, disallowing vacations and interrupting day activities. When chore time comes, one has to leave. My grandmother, even late in life when she lived in town, used to imitate a neighbor, saying " I've got to go home now and feed my 'kashaw'." Years later I realized her acknowledgement of daily chores referred to a pig. Her neighbor had brought along a remnant of French when he came down from Quebec and he was saying "couchon" -pig.

Lines Written on the Eve of Surgery

Winter, coming on swiftly as it did that year,
Caught my neighbor's spreader in its icy jaws,
Freezing gear and wheel and slider boards
That would not move again 'til spring.
The relentless gutter cleaner daily brought
More sorrow and manure to the trapped device
And filled the bay with a debt to be paid
With dung fork and muscle in late spring.

Now come I to swift winter,
Threatening even as the jonquils fade:
Unwritten letters, unread books, unvisited friends,
Unfinished scraps of ideas, untaught beauty,
And unsaid love pile into the shortage of time,
With no guarantee of thaw to release mind and vigor
 Into the digging.

I'm glad I never scoffed at my neighbor's
Sad, winter-grasped, shit spreader,
Buried in its task.

Going for Sawdust

We had gathered at the home of a friend to celebrate the end of winter. The old house – an original structure of the once Victorian town – glowed within from lamps and candles, casting a warm light on brocade walls, paisley throws and the faces of our wives. I enjoyed this ambience awhile, but soon sought out a friend of mine. He and I always had interesting conversations, but this night I wanted to tell him about the disaster the weather had wrought upon the pasture fence I built the previous summer. Heavy snows in December, followed by an ice storm in January, followed by snow upon snow after that, had stacked up trouble for my fence. It only needed this spring thaw to bring it down, barbwire and all. I was a "pretend" farmer, raising a couple of beef critters and a summer pig, while relying on a job in town for my livelihood. My friend, on the other hand, is a real farmer with a large dairy herd. He would understand my distress and give me more sympathy than my friends from town.

We found each other by the bourbon and mixes on the kitchen counter and, after a "What'll you have?" and a "How was your day?" he reeled out a saga about going for sawdust.

The sideboards were already on, so about mid-day he set out. He had seen that Garland Hill was dry enough and he surmised that the drive over to McIndoes would be equally fair. Unfortunately, large portions of the road lay in shaded cuts where mud season was in full progress. Second gear and dual

wheels carried him through but he determined to bring his load home by another way.

At Woodsville, he discovered that the saws and blower were down and that the funnel hopper was empty. He knew he would have to go on to Newbury and load by hand. He rued his decision to leave his two strong boys at home.

At the Newbury mill, the recent digging had eroded a kerf in the pile just big enough let one truck back in. "When I got out and looked at that wall behind the truck", he said, "I could see, in the layers of sawdust and snow, the history of the mill activity and the weather for the entire winter. Anyway, I got about half loaded when another truck arrived and a young farmer- late twenties or so- got out and helped me finish my load. The courtesy is to turn-about and so you see we had time to talk."

"We told about our farms: how many milking head, who we were shipping to, and so on. He said he was working his father's farm and I casually asked what the arrangements were. Was he getting a salary? Was he getting a percentage of the milk check? He said he was working for promised equity in the farm. To me, farming is a business and this didn't sound like good business. I should have let it go at that but I probed a little further and asked if he had a written agreement." 'No.' he said. "By that time a whole torrent of business anxiety was rushing into my head and I asked him if he had any brothers or sisters. He pondered the intention of that question a bit before answering." 'Yes, but they would never contest my right to the farm.' "I got right into it then and tried to explain the advantages - the necessity – of having a written contract."

"The more I talked, the quieter he became. I tried to clarify my position. Then I tried to undo the perceived offense, but the more I talked, the more tight-lipped he became. The more agitated he became, the more I stumbled over my words. You know how long it has taken me to be able to say 'Bennington, Brattleboro, Banana Belt' without stuttering, but it was all out the window. Finally I gave up, and we shoveled on in silence."

"When it was done, (It seemed like hours later.), he heaved his shovel up onto the load and turned to me and growled 'I think if I went over to your farm, I could find something wrong with *it.*' "He climbed up into his cab and drove off without covering his load."

"I decided to go home by way of Groton and South Peacham. A dusting of sawdust marked the trail of the other truck until a wide crescent of sawdust in the road showed where he had turned off into the stony uplands of West Ryegate."

"When I came up the road to home I could see the lights on in the barn and knew the boys had started chores. Good boys! They were almost done with the milking so I showered up and wife and I came to the party, pretty much on time."

"You know, we must have made a comical sight up there on the top of the sawdust pile with our silhouettes against the late day sky; He, in stony silence, jabbing his shovel into the pile like a highland warrior swinging a claymore, and I, gesturing and stammering and struggling to present my advice as friendly concern rather than arrogant judgment. But to me it wasn't funny. I like to be known for who I am and, I suppose that young farmer does too. We both lost out today."

"Maybe", I said, "but everyone here knows who you are and I haven't heard any complaints." He knew it was a compliment. I looked at our empty glasses and said "can I fix you another?'

I forgot to tell him about my fence.

Apple Blossoms

The snow that fell before its time
And lingered into April's early days
Released, at last, its grip upon the knurly trunk
And shrunk to dirty mounds beneath the densest firs.
Now in gentler grasp,
The tree again stands ringed in white,
The pale precipitate of its broken blossoms.
Each wind,
Servant to the law that all must be scattered,
Brings down another flurry.
One can as easily stop the snow from falling
As these petals
Which, a week ago, were formed among new leaves.
Time goes toward disorder,
But I, more than time's arrow
Must take the blame for hastening the spring.
I wished each moment into one more wonderful
And, astonished gazed
Until the blushing flowers fell away.
Spring, of all seasons, ought to be savored
For time, without urging will hasten into winter,
And winters here are very long.

Avis, Champion

I was named after my aunt
But I was convinced,
As the I only blonde
Among my parents' redheaded offspring,
That I was adopted.
Convinced, that is, until we all began to run.
In high school cross-country, skiing and track
We were serious contenders against area schools,
But the competition began when we were young;
Racing each other across our meadow
To the swimming hole,
We seemed to be related,
-At least in the ability to run.
My mother ruled that swimming could not start
Until her mid-June birthday,
No matter how hot the days.
By then the timothy and June-grass was up
In the meadow, and my father forbade crossing it;
"It'll look like a truck route
After you've tromped it all down.
Might as well grow vetch."
So we trudged down to the corner
To splash in the shallow water
While dreaming of the slow, deep brook
Behind the barrier of sacred hay.
Some time in July -late, it seemed to us -
The neighbor came with all his equipment
And put the hay in the barn,
Leaving behind a field of
Stubble.

Racing and swimming season was finally on,
And my stubble-crushing, snake-stomping,
Thistle-defying feet were ready.
Though we all grew to be "best at" many things,
It was important when I was ten for me to be
Best at the Barn to Brook Barefoot Dash.
Tackling and tumbling,
My brother and sister impeded each other.
My father, obedient to my mother's edict of
"No shoes down by the brook",
Ouch, ouched his way in distant last place.
I sprinted ahead and was first in the cool water;
A champion runner in a family of runners.

Backswath

The summer before I went off to college, I decided that my employment should be outdoors in the sunshine and fresh air: Haying. My labor was to augment that of the full-time hired man, - a fellow who was two or three years older than I.

Room and board at the farm was counted as bonus, but only meant that I was to be a participant in morning and evening chores. The "work" was in the hayfield.

Like most families of my teen years, mine provided for me but it was not a democracy. I knew who sat at the head of the table and made the rules. Therefore, I was not troubled by the hierarchy evident on the first drive out to the hayfield when Stanley took the wheel and the boss waited for me to get in and straddle the shifter while he rode in the place of honor. This served me well when I worked at a ready-mix batch plant and could discern which chair in the lunchroom belonged to the boss

If the weather had been benevolent, the hay was cut, raked and ready to bale. The boss took over the tractor/baler/buncher, and Stanley and I took over the old restructured bread truck. Stanley and I agreed to swap loading and driving responsibilities sequentially. Fair in most aspects except he manipulated the series so as to ensure that I was loading the backswath.

In order to obtain clearance for the baler, the first turn around the hayfield by the side delivery rake has to go in the "wrong" direction, pulling a content of partially dried hay, swailgrass and sticks away from

the alders. In addition, the first "right" direction pushes a second windrow into the first, making the combined windrow doubly thick. There in the shade of trees that dense ribbon never seemed to dry.

The normal bale weighs about 40 lbs in the hayfield, but the "bricks" made from the backswath weigh at least twice as much –objects loathed by the loader. I once rolled one into the brook to see if it would float. It snagged in the shallow water and foiled my experiment.

I would rate loading the backswath as one of the most odious tasks on the farm, but I later changed my mind.

A few years after my farming summer, some bright person – a farmer, I suspect – got the idea that hay would dry a lot faster if the awns were crushed to let out some of the moisture. He may have gathered the idea from watching his wife's old time washer with the abutting rubber cylinders called a clothes wringer. The device hastened the drying of everything hung out on the clothesline. Eureka! A wringer for the hayfield called a conditioner!

We didn't have a conditioner.

It takes 3 or 4 good drying days for hay to make. A perverse June can produce rain every third day, making a destructive sequence of wet, nearly dry, wet, nearly dry and so on that makes a blackened, ruined hay. By using a conditioner to save a day of drying, haymakers were able circumvent the frequent rains and get the hay into bales and off to the barn.

When hay got wet in the fifties, new strategies were required. Another turnover by the side delivery rake might help. Some farmers had tedders, towed machines that had several flailing tines that flung the hay into the air. Our farmer had 2 young hired men with pitchforks go around and around the windrows shaking out the hay. Tedious and callous-producing, but not heavy, this labor barely achieved drying before the next rain, The farmer's anxiety began to border on insanity. He accused us of having "a guitar lesson" when we paused to discus the next direction for our load. Once when we had the field ready to go, the baler broke a shear pin. No spare. Luckily, the boss had driven his Packard out to the field that day and he roared off toward town. We heard the trooper's siren just after he went out of site. When he returned, he said to us, "It was a good thing he caught me when he did, I was planning to do a hundred when I got to the straightaway".

In spite of terrible weather, we managed to finish haying in mid July and hoped to rest until the rowan crop. That was a dream. A neighbor decided to retire from the egg production business. He also decided to raze the two-story henhouse so his wife could enjoy the long obscured view of the river. He gave the contents —nitrogen rich droppings – to our boss. for his fallow field. "Corn will grow tall in that free fertilizer". Free, except that Stanley and I had to shovel it out.

In September I left, mid rowan for college in Boston thinking there could be nothing worse than backswath bales, wet hay and hen manure. I encountered a sadistic course called "Logic" delivered by a stubby Hungarian refugee with two gray dresses and no command of the English language. I longed to be back on the farm.

Post script note: I sent this story to my friend, Peacham dairy farmer George Kempton. His return letter contained this interesting recollection of his own younger days in the hayfield; "The backswath is a product of the side delivery rake. In 1945 I worked on a farm in the hills of Windsor Vermont. It had been held back by the war and location and they farmed very much as they had in the twenties. We raked with a dump rake, tumbled, and pitched on by hand. Two of the jobs that I did as the boy on the farm that are rarely done now are: pull a bull rake while they were pitching on, to make sure no spear of hay was lost, and mow with a scythe along the brook, woods and fence lines to ensure that no brush could grow. As I look back on it, perhaps having a backswath is not a bad trade ".

Avatar –A Fable

In dreary Januarys. some years before television and long before the movie "Avatar", parents in the local PTA organized a yearly stage show about avatars. There was a war taking place, and though Jack Benny brought a few laughs to the radio and the Lone Ranger entertained youngsters, much of what came from the speakers began with "There's sad news tonight". A show that could temporarily distract worried families and brighten a few winter evenings, seemed like a good thing. As avatars, the older men could hide their various singing talent in a chorus and tell corny jokes about their neighbors with impunity. The jokes were sometimes embarrassing moments remembered about community members during the past year, but more often they were from "Eastman's Chestnuts" or other joke books, One man in the men's group was appointed as chief facilitator and jokes were introduced to him by one or another of the chorus, "Mister Interlocutor, did you hear about…." Mothers and older sisters taking part in the revelry shunned the grease paint, preferring to put on lipstick and pretty dresses, imitating Southern belles. Many of the songs were from the Stephen Foster songbook.

Non-avatar talent was also featured: Mrs. Brown, had played piano for silent movies and could bring every human emotion to life on the keys. Reverend Horsefield sang "On the road to Mandalay, Where the flying fishes play, Where the sun comes up like thunderrr out of China 'cross the bay…" Servicemen, if home on leave, would sing a rousing patriotic song or two. An avatar from the chorus, attired in yellow-painted shoes did a tap dance and sang "Oh them golden slippers, golden slippers I'm going to wear to climb the golden stairs."

Eventually, the avatars came to live among us through the medium of television, and people saw that the portrayals were offensive. They shifted to "Hee-Haw" type shows for a while, but "I Love Lucy" and "The Honeymooners" soon eclipsed the home-grown talent,

Years later, under a cigar box of 6 penny nails I found my father's make-up kit with its mustaches, wigs, grease paint, Ponds Face Cream and charcoal sticks. I dumped it out and kept the box. There was a piece of broadside in the bottom. It announced a minstrel show at the Arlington School.

The Shay

The carriage was almost in the road
As was the snow-crushed barn
From which it had been rescued.
Leaves rotting on the floor
And four wheel rims sunk into the soil
Showed seasons of neglect.
I thought it restorable
And a lucky find
After a day of wandering country roads
Looking for blueberries
While empty pails rattled in the back.
I'm grateful that I never had to contend
With harnesses and equine temperament,
But I admired my brother's horses
And here was a worthy complement
To the sleigh I had given him
Some years before.
Up here, half the year is winter
But snowy lanes suitable for a sleigh ride
Are quickly salted and sanded
To make them into summerlike roads
For automobiles.
A shay like this one would be useful
More days of the year.

My stopping brought forth an old man
From the nearby house
Who immediately began to extol the virtues
Of this decaying wagon.
"He wants to elevate the price," I thought.

But I have learned a thing or two about dealing
So I let him go on, singing up an imagined buggy.
Like a scene from "Oklahoma".
A wheelwright could restore the rims.
The rodent-chewed button-tuck seats
Could be reupholstered in a bright fabric.
The moldy floor and missing dash
Could be replaced with plywood
And lined with carpet.
The tangle of rods that once held up a roof
Could be removed to make a sleeker model.
It would be a fine rig.

But no, he wouldn't sell it at any price.
His grandchildren might come next summer
And they would be proud to sit up there
With Granddad and maybe hold the reins.
I saw no evidence of horse or stable,
But who am I to splash reality on a dream.
I thanked him and rattled on down to Lisbon
To make something of the day
By buying a few used books
And a cup of coffee.

Habakkuk

My uncle cried when the late-summer hail
shredded all his tall corn and left it a as a tangled
wreckage, fit only for plowing under. It wasn't the
corn only; he had recently boarded a "five thousand
dollar bull" that had brought brucellosis and a torrent
of veterinary bills upon his herd. And just a few weeks
before the hailstorm, when we were haying late for a
widowed neighbor, his wife of three decades fell and
broke her wrist. Her pain, unaided because of our
delay, stirred up all her harbored frustrations so when
we returned she was gone, not to return for many
years. My job as hired man expanded to include
cooking – cause enough for tears in itself. Yet, in a
summer of rain and calamity we managed to get hay in
the barn and milk in the cooler.

I marveled that my uncle had the will to rise and
face each day, but he did so and with positive strength
receptive to the good he might find in it. He was glad
for the coffee I rose early to make; glad to see his
three-story barn floating in the morning fog like a great
ship: glad to hear the swallows twittering in its cupola:
glad to hear the baseball scores on the radio (more so if
the Red Sox had done well); glad to husband his big
Ayrshires.

Though remote in time and place from my uncle's
New Hampshire farm, the prophet Habakkuk was
similarly able to transcend the portent of agricultural
disaster and proclaim "I will joy in the God of my
salvation."

Lord, likewise grant to us the strength to rise above the pervasive chaos and see the good in each new day.

Bruce Hoyt decidedly North of Brattleboro
on a visit to Alaska.